THE REFUGEE'S BILLIONAIRE

RACHELLE J. CHRISTENSEN

Peachwood Press

Praise for

Rachelle J. Christensen's
Award-winning Novels

Hawaiian Masquerade is the perfect summer read. Set on the beautiful island of Kauai, you will fall in love with the characters, the story line, the setting, and most of all the romance. I would highly recommend this fast-paced, fabulous clean romance.

--Cami Checketts, author of *The Feisty One: A Billionaire Bride Pact Romance*

Christensen has done a magnificent job of putting together an unlikely match and letting it challenge the characters to grow, change, and become better together than they were apart. This is a wonderful, sweet romance that you'll want to stay up to finish.

-Lucy McConnell, author of the *Billionaire Marriage Brokers* series

"SILVER CASCADE SECRETS is an exciting romantic suspense novella ... Great writing, a sweet romance, and an intriguing mystery all rolled into a single story."

—Heather B. Moore *USA Today* Bestselling Author of *Finding Sheba*

"Just in time for fall, ... romantic suspense which will tingle the spine and thrill the heart."
—DESERET NEWS, Melissa Demoux

"...A great read for a lazy Sunday afternoon. I highly recommend."
—Diane Darcy, USA Today bestselling author

"Don't expect to get a lot of sleep...If the thrills of the chase don't get you, the thrills of the heart will."
—J. Scott Savage, author of the Mysteries of Cove Series

"*Diamond Rings are Deadly Things* pulled me right in from the first page and held me captive until the very end. Great characters, a compelling plot, a surprising twist at the end... Rachelle Christensen knows how to craft a great mystery."
—*Tristi Pinkston, author of the Secret Sisters Mysteries*

ALSO BY RACHELLE J. CHRISTENSEN

Diamond Rings Are Deadly Things (Wedding Planner Mysteries #1)

Veils and Vengeance (#2)

Proposals and Poison (#3)

The Soldier's Bride (A Music Box Romance #1)

Carve Me a Melody (A Music Box Romance #2)

Hawaiian Masquerade (Burke Billionaire Romance #1)

The Billionaire's Stray Heart (Burke Billionaire Romance #2)

The Refugee's Billionaire (Burke Billionaire Romance #3)

How to Fetch a Fiancé

River Whispers

Hope for Christmas: An Echo Ridge Romance #1

The Kiss Thief: An Echo Ridge Romance #2

The Princess Bride of Riodan: An Echo Ridge Romance #3

Coming Home to Love: An Echo Ridge Romance #4

Her Guy Next Door Fake Fiancé: Echo Ridge Romance #5

Novellas:

Silver Cascade Secrets

Double Take

Claire's Christmas Dance

Nonfiction:

What Every 6th Grader Needs to Know: 10

Secrets to Connect Moms & Daughters

Lost Children: Coping with Miscarriage

This is a work of fiction, and the views expressed herein are the sole responsibility of the author. Likewise, certain characters, places, and incidents are the product of the author's imagination, and any resemblance to actual persons, living or dead, or actual events or locales, is entirely coincidental.

Copyright © 2018 Peachwood Press LLC

All rights reserved.

Original Cover Design: Peachwood Design

Cover Design: Steven Novak

Edited by: Precision Editing Group

No part of this book may be reproduced in any form or by any means without permission in writing from the publisher, except for the inclusion of brief quotations in a review.

ISBN 13:978-1-949319-13-2

Published by Peachwood Press, LLC November 2018

 Created with Vellum

Get your free book!

Thrills for the Heart

FOR A LIMITED TIME

Sign up for Rachelle's
VIP Mailing List
to get your *FREE* book.

★ ★ ★ ★ ★

Get started here:
www.rachellechristensen.com

Carolina Diaz opened the kitchen window across from the stove in the refugee center. The balmy air trickled in, caressing her skin. February in Atlanta, Georgia, was a lovely time. It wasn't too cold, and the humidity was at a bearable level. *Maybe I'll have time to take Daniel outside today,* she thought. But first, there was a long list of tasks that needed completed, and Carolina was excited about her work that day. It was a busy day for a Tuesday, and everyone worked hard to meet the goals the refugee center had set.

Pots and pans clanked behind her as several volunteers worked to prepare lunch for the refugees who had arrived last week to the Heart of Atlanta Refugee Center. She straightened and looked around the room. The center was one place where Carolina always felt like she belonged.

Carolina lifted her right hand, studying the gold band with bits of rubies embedded along one side. It had belonged to her grandmother, and Carolina still felt an ache in her chest when memories of simpler times surfaced. Five years ago Carolina and her grandmother had arrived in America. At the young age of sixteen she had fled Cuba, seeking a new life with her grandmother. Through the kindness of volunteers in this very center, Carolina was living the life her grandmother had hoped for before she passed away.

Carolina carried a stack of plates to the serving area, and then poked her head out of the kitchen to where she had last seen her son, Daniel, playing. Only four years old, her precocious little boy needed the eyes of every volunteer in the center to keep him out of trouble. She looked across the hall where refugee families gathered in an open area for games, crafts, and learning skills to help them acclimate to America. Daniel was driving a wooden car across the tile floor, crawling after it and making motor sounds. It was one of hundreds that a volunteer had made for children who showed up with nothing but the shirts on their backs. A few of her volunteer friends smiled and waved when they saw Carolina checking on Daniel.

Carolina smiled at her son. She was about to turn back into the kitchen, when she noticed a man walk through the entryway, carrying a leather shoulder bag. A *very* fine man. He was dressed in a business suit with a blue silk tie. His beard was trimmed close. He appeared to be in his thirties, but as the man walked toward a group of people filling out paperwork on a table, Carolina guessed that he was only a few years older than her, maybe in his mid-twenties. He pushed a hand through his thick black hair as he surveyed the center. He definitely didn't fit in with the ragtag crew that haunted the center.

The man must have felt her stare. He caught her eye, and the side of his mouth lifted in a hesitant smile. Daniel chose that moment to drive his car over the man's shoes, and motored around in a circle. As the man crouched next to her son, Carolina took a step forward, intent on helping Daniel apologize.

"Hola. ¿Cómo estás?" the man said in a deep voice she could barely hear from across the room.

Daniel looked up and smiled. "Bien." He gave his car a push, and it banged against the wall, one wheel popping off. Daniel frowned and plopped down on his bottom. "It broke!"

He started crying, but the man put his hand tenderly on Daniel's back. "Hey, I can fix it." Carolina walked toward her son hesitantly. How was this attractive businessman in his immaculate suit going to soothe Daniel's tears?

He picked up the car and the wheel, blew on the wheel, and snapped it back into place. He pushed the car, and it rolled forward across the tile. "See, it just needed a little magic."

"Gracias," Daniel said and scooted after the car.

Carolina laughed as she walked the last few steps toward her son. The man stood and smiled at her. "Can you believe this kid? They said all these refugees have arrived in the last two weeks, but his English is great."

"That's because he's an American," Carolina replied, her lips twitching with laughter.

The man turned to her. His eyes matched the color of his blue silk tie. "Huh? What do you mean?"

"He's my son. I work here."

"Oh, you're not—"

"Carolina Diaz." She held out her hand. "I came to America as a refugee to this very center five years ago. My son was born here in Georgia." Her speech was still edged with a Spanish accent, but at least people didn't have to strain to understand her anymore. The handsome man in front of her didn't seem to be struggling. "Where did you learn to speak Spanish?"

Shawn chuckled. "I don't think counting to ten and saying a few greetings counts as speaking a language, but I did study some in college." He took her hand and gave it a firm shake. "I'm Shawn Halstrom from Burke Enterprises. I'm here in regards to a possible donation that Lexi and Jordan Burke want to make to a center in this area."

A donation? It must be the one Lisette had hinted at

—the one that could keep the center running. "Oh, from Burke's Higher Steps. That's wonderful," Carolina said, trying to ignore the tingle that went up her arm at his touch. "Have you met our director, Lisette Douglas?" She checked his left hand—no ring, so this man was a single and very wealthy man. Too bad she'd sworn off dating.

Shawn nodded. "I was in yesterday, and she showed me around. I'll be meeting with her again today."

Carolina hadn't worked the day before because she'd taken Daniel to the dentist. How high up was Shawn in the Burke's Higher Steps foundation? Would he be the sole decision-maker for the donation? "Well, last I saw, she was in the kitchen checking on supplies. Would you like to wait in her office, and I'll tell her you're here?"

"Sure. She's expecting me, but I can work on a few things if she needs to finish up."

Shawn didn't seem like the type who was used to waiting for others, but his smile seemed genuine. Lisette had told her about the people behind Burke's Higher Steps. They were all billionaires. Was Shawn a billionaire then? Did he have the power to single-handedly change the fate of their center? Nerves gripped the outside of Carolina's shoulders as Shawn followed her to Lisette's office. Carolina hesitated in the doorway, wanting to ask him what he thought of the center; instead she swallowed her curiosity. "Okay, I'll be back in a few."

Carolina hurried back through the kitchen and located Lisette. The tall, dark-skinned woman held a clipboard and was pointing at a stack of cans with her pencil, probably mentally counting how many they would need for the next week. "Hey, Lisette. There's a man named Shawn here, something to do with Burke Enterprises."

Lisette turned, and her brown eyes lit up with a smile. "Oh, I'm glad you met him. He's such a nice guy. What did you think of him?"

Carolina raised an eyebrow. "He's a wealthy businessman who wants to make sure we're using funds correctly. What's to think?" There was a lot to think, but she didn't want her boss to know anything about how attractive she thought Shawn was or how kind he'd been to Daniel.

Lisette clucked her tongue. "Oh, he's not what you think. Shawn has soul—have you seen those blue eyes of his?"

"I didn't really notice. I was checking on Daniel." Carolina looked down at the floor. Hopefully Lisette wouldn't notice the flush of her cheeks. She *had* noticed Shawn's blue eyes, and she hadn't wanted to look away. "Anyway, he's waiting for you in your office."

"Great," Lisette replied. "I think this donation could be the difference-maker we've been praying for." She tucked a black strand of hair back into the bun at the nape of her neck.

"Oh?" They both had big dreams for the center. Lisette wanted to offer more for those arriving in such a tumultuous time of their life. One of those dreams involved Carolina setting up a skills center to teach marketable skills to the refugees. Many of them could not read, write, or speak English. If they could get a sizable donation, Lisette hoped to provide job training for the refugees. Carolina also wanted to work with the existing talents that many refugees learned in their homeland to craft a living for themselves in America.

"Yes, that's why Shawn is here—to identify exactly how much we need."

"You mean they're going to donate whatever we need?" Carolina couldn't keep her mouth from dropping open.

"Well, not exactly like that, but," Lisette tilted one hand from side to side, "if they choose to help our center, it will be an incredibly generous donation. Lexi and her brother Jordan are wonderful people. Everyone at Burke's Higher Steps is fabulous."

Carolina grinned. "That's the best news I've heard all day."

"Why don't you come in to the meeting with Shawn?" Lisette asked.

"Oh, no, I couldn't. I probably wouldn't understand half of what you say." And she would probably get caught staring at Shawn's blue eyes instead of listening.

Lisette paused and put her hand on Carolina's shoulder. "You can do more than you know, Carolina. Don't hide your talents."

"I'll work on that, but right now I'd better go check

on Daniel." Carolina turned and hurried out of the kitchen. Lisette always encouraged her, but life had been kinder to her than it had been to Carolina. Still, what talents did she think that Carolina had to offer the center?

"We both know he's just fine," Lisette called, teasing laughter in her voice.

Carolina couldn't help but smile as she crossed the hall to check on her son. She also couldn't help but notice Shawn sitting next to Lisette's desk typing on his phone. He looked up as she passed and smiled, those blue eyes lighting up with interest. Ducking her head, Carolina walked purposefully toward the multipurpose room. *Think of Daniel, not of Shawn and his blue eyes,* she thought.

❧   2   ❧

Shawn stared after the woman with the dark brown curls. She was gorgeous, and he had to resist the urge to lean forward in his chair as she walked by. He wanted to know her story. It was fascinating that she had been a refugee and now worked at the center. That was exactly the kind of information that his boss, Jordan Burke, and his boss's sister, Lexi, had tasked him to collect on this trip. His boss made up one half of the brother-sister team of Burke Enterprises housed in the booming city of Chicago, Illinois. Right about now, Shawn didn't miss the breakneck speed of the Burke office, and he definitely didn't miss the chilling temperatures in Chicago. Atlanta's weather was temperate and beautiful, and even though the city was large, the population was not even a fourth the size of Chicago. Atlanta seemed to have a different pace. Shawn couldn't put his finger on it; maybe it was something to do with the South. Maybe he could ask Carolina about that. He shook his head and refocused on his notes.

Over the next few weeks, Shawn would make visits and work with other employees at the refugee center to discover exactly what Burke's Higher Steps could do to help make a difference in a big way. Shawn heard someone in the hall and straightened, hoping to catch a glimpse of the woman he'd met earlier, Carolina. Stupid that a woman was turning his head right now. He hadn't had time for a relationship in years, but it had been a long time since he'd seen a woman that stunning. She'd said her name with a Spanish accent, *Cahroleena*. Shawn's heart thumped hard in his chest when he caught sight of Carolina leading her young son by the hand. No wedding ring that he could see. He hoped that meant she was single.

Her little boy had darker skin than his mother, and his black hair was cut short. He seemed to be happy at the center, and by the looks of it, he was here whenever his mother was working. If Shawn could interview Carolina, she could give him great insight into the life of a refugee and how to successfully acclimate into a new country and culture. She might be able to help him understand more about the center from her unique point of view. It was his job to find out, wasn't it?

He shook his head. Why was he thinking about the beautiful single mother? He had no experience with kids, and Carolina probably didn't even remember his name. Still, working at the center might present an opportunity to learn more about her—maybe there was a chance, however slim.

"Nice to see you again, Shawn," Lisette said as she walked into her office.

Shawn stood quickly and shook her hand. "Thanks for meeting with me again. I've been going over the expense reports and I have a few questions."

For the next twenty minutes, Shawn peppered Lisette with questions about the resources used to keep the center running. Yesterday he'd made the snap judgement that the Heart of Atlanta was very lucky to have Lisette Douglas running the center. Today he reiterated that judgement, happy that he was able to work with someone competent and trustworthy.

"Lisette, I appreciate this info. It's going to make my job a lot easier. You've done well to come up with creative ideas to stretch your dollars." And he hadn't thought about Carolina for almost twenty minutes.

Lisette smiled. "Thank you, but I can't take all the credit. The secretary over allocations is incredibly bright and keeps the center running on a tight budget."

"Really? I'd like to meet with her. I'm supposed to speak with several personnel who might be involved in spending the proposed donation from Burke's Higher Steps."

Lisette grinned and her eyes twinkled. "I was hoping

you'd say that. I'll be right back." She stood and scooted out of her office.

A couple minutes later, Lisette returned with Carolina Diaz. Her eyes widened when Shawn stood, and he thought he noticed her cheeks darken with a blush. "We meet again."

"Oh, that's right. You've already met," Lisette said. Shawn wasn't sure, but he thought he saw her wink at Carolina. "I was just telling Shawn what a wonderful job you've done in coming up with unique ways to make each dollar go further in our center."

Carolina ducked her head, and Shawn knew he was in trouble. It had been a long time since he'd met a shy woman. Most of the ones he'd interacted with over the past few years were more on the brazen side and it had made it easier for him to swear off women.

He cleared his throat. "Would you mind sitting with me for a few minutes and going over a few of the ideas I've discussed with Lisette?" Shawn watched her slowly lift her head and meet his eyes.

"Okay." She sat in the chair next to him.

"I have to run and sign for a delivery," Lisette said. "Please, go on without me. Carolina is more than qualified to share her thoughts."

Carolina looked after Lisette with a sort of desperate worry before turning back to Shawn. "I'm not sure if I'm the best person to answer your questions, but I'll try."

Her Spanish accent colored each word with an exotic

spice that made Shawn's mouth water. He pulled his eyes away from her and concentrated on his notebook. "Why don't you tell me about one of your favorite ideas?"

"Okay." Carolina bit her bottom lip and furrowed her brow, but then she looked up and smiled, her brow relaxing. "Instead of using all the money the state gave us for new books, I organized a book drive, specifically asking for books written in Spanish."

"Really? But I thought the idea of the books was to teach the refugees English."

"Sí. I mean, yes. Many people who come here don't read well. Or if they can read, it's only in their native language, not English. If they feel comfortable reading in their native tongue, they are more willing to expand into a different language."

"I see. Your English is wonderful, by the way. Did you know how to speak any English before you came to America?"

Carolina shook her head. "None, but my grand-mother was determined that I learn to speak it and speak it well."

"That's wonderful. So what did you do with the money allocated to books?"

Carolina straightened. "We purchased some training manuals with detailed illustrations to help teach and expand skills that many of the refugees could use to get a job. We also bought a matching English book for every Spanish book that was donated. Spanish isn't the only language spoken by refugees in Atlanta, but the majority of the people who come to this center do speak Spanish."

"That's some smart thinking. I like it, Carolina," Shawn said. "I'd like to run some ideas past you and see if you have a different take on them."

"Oh, okay," she replied, looking at him uncertainly.

Her long hair trailed over her shoulders. She twisted it and pushed it to one side, exposing the smooth skin of her neck. Shawn met her eyes and realized that he'd been staring too long. She averted her eyes in a move that left him wondering what had happened in her life to steal her confidence.

The next day, Carolina was scheduled to work at the refugee center early so she packed a bag with books and toys for Daniel. They caught the bus, and on the ride over she tried not to think about Shawn Halstrom and the way he had assessed her, those blue eyes admiring her but not in the leering way she had grown accustomed to from so many men.

When Carolina arrived in a strange place with her grandmother, she had tried to find her way in the new world of America, but at sixteen she knew next to nothing about how the real world worked. Her grandmother had been slowly fighting a cancer that they didn't see until it was too late. Carolina was left to fend for herself; unfortunately, she fell for the leering gaze of a young man who knew his way around too many naïve young women. When she got pregnant, she discovered the truth about the man she thought she loved.

Daniel held one of his cars in his hand and looked out the window to the busy street. She couldn't imagine life without Daniel. Her heart had never fully recovered from the shock of falling in love with the wrong man, but it was okay because she'd turned her heart over to God. The missionaries that came by her grandmother's apartment talked of a loving God, a forgiving God, one who would never abandon His sheep. Carolina had clung to those words as she had clung to her newborn baby. She'd clung to those words as her grandmother slipped away from the earth. Carolina wasn't even a legal adult, but she was an orphan and a mother, and she was desperate for help.

The Heart of Atlanta Refugee Center had been her saving grace. She had returned to the first safe place she'd ever known since leaving her home country of Cuba. Lisette had placed her with several volunteers who helped her get a GED and trained her in secretarial work at the center.

Carolina put her arm around Daniel and smiled down at him. He pushed a matchbox car along the edge of the bus seat making motor noises, and then he stopped and grinned up at his mother. "Hi Mommy. I'm going to drive my car today again with Shawn."

"Oh, you think so?" Her son remembered Shawn

from the brief interaction the day before? Unless— "Did you play with Shawn again yesterday?"

"Yeah, he makes the cars go really fast!" Daniel made a motor noise again and held his car up in the air.

Carolina's heart hitched in her chest with a feeling that was unfamiliar yet pleasant. Shawn had been so gentle with Daniel when her son had been on the verge of a tantrum. She swallowed a giggle, remembering how Shawn had thought Daniel couldn't speak English. She gave her head a little shake. She needed to stop thinking about Shawn. He was obviously well-educated and far out of her league. Besides, he lived halfway across the United States in Chicago. In a week or so, he would leave, and she would never see him again.

After Daniel was settled with a puzzle and a few snacks, Carolina sat at her desk and got to work. She'd learned to type quickly, and that had helped improve her English—a skill that made her doubly valuable to the center. She was able to converse in her native Spanish language and also translate into English.

Lisette breezed into the room, a stack of folders in her arms. "Good morning, Carolina. I have something I need your help with. Do you have a few minutes?"

Carolina glanced at Daniel, who was watching Curious George on the TV, and nodded. "Sure, what did you need?"

Lisette brightened. "Come this way." She led Carolina

out of the front office and into the multipurpose room. Carolina's stomach flipped when she saw Shawn standing near a table covered with papers. He wore a finely tailored gray suit, and he leaned forward to examine a stack of papers. The suit fit him just right. She slowed and hissed at Lisette, "What are you doing?"

"This is what I needed help with. I asked Shawn if he'd be willing to work with you to flesh out the ideas we've come up with for the skills center and job-training department. He thought it was a great idea." Lisette stopped and turned toward Carolina. "Have a little faith in yourself, and don't be afraid of Shawn. He's a good man. He won't hurt you."

Carolina nodded. "Okay." She followed Lisette toward Shawn. He looked up, his eyes finding hers. The skin around his eyes crinkled. He seemed genuinely happy to see her.

"Morning. Glad you could help me today." Shawn motioned to the stack of papers spread out on the table. "Lisette wasn't kidding when she said this would take some work."

Lisette chuckled. "I think you'll find that Carolina has a creative way of looking at things that will help you get things sorted. I want you two to work together for the rest of the week."

Oh no. It was fine to ogle his business suit from afar, but if she had to spend hours working right next to

Shawn, how would she hide her interest? "But what about my other work?" She couldn't lose her job at the center. It was all she had. There weren't many places that would allow her to bring her son to work with her.

"Don't worry, hon," Lisette said. "If you can come in thirty minutes early each day and do the urgent tasks, everything else can wait. We need to get this sorted out, and I'm confident you're the right person to help Shawn do just that."

Carolina swallowed and looked from Lisette to Shawn. If she didn't need the extra money, she might've chickened out. "Okay, I'll try my best."

"You always do." Lisette patted her on the back and left the room.

"Lisette has nothing but good to say about you, Carolina. Don't look so worried," Shawn said.

Her heart stood at attention when Shawn said her name, placing emphasis on the long "e" sound, the way her grandmother used to. She studied him for a moment. He had an open, honest face and he was there to work, just like her. "What would you like me to do?"

Shawn pulled up two chairs and sat beside her as he began going over budget sheets and possible allocations for a new department. "Tell me what your vision is for this area." Shawn waved his arm in front of them, indicating the large room.

Carolina leaned back in her chair, squinting slightly as

her creative vision filled in the space in front of her. "We need tables, bookshelves, laptops, art supplies, crafting materials, and bins to keep everything in. Most of the refugees coming in from Cuba or Africa have wonderful hand-working skills. If we could get them the materials to produce crafts, they could sell their creations at the local farmer's market or some of the flea markets nearby."

"But do you have access to the kind of materials they know how to work with?"

"I'm still looking into that, but yes, I think we can get what they need." Carolina refocused on Shawn. She'd been carried away with her vision for the center. What if he thought it sounded ridiculous?

Shawn tilted his head and smiled. "I like this idea. It's perfect."

"Thanks." Carolina felt a thrill of excitement when she noticed the genuine admiration on Shawn's face. Better control her beating heart.

"Where's your son today?" Shawn asked.

Carolina motioned to the offices behind them. "He's watching cartoons in the other room. I'm very lucky that everyone here at the center loves Daniel and helps take care of him."

Shawn nodded. "The people here, they are good people." He licked his lips. "So, I didn't notice a ring. Are you a single mother?"

Any chance she'd had at impressing him just plummeted. Carolina lowered her head. "I've never been married."

"Hey," Shawn leaned closer and touched her arm. "I'm sorry if I made you feel uncomfortable. I just wanted to get to know you better."

Carolina lifted her head and met his gaze. There was nothing in his eyes that suggested judgment or disappointment in what she had confessed. "Daniel is my anchor in life. He brought me to God. It's because of him that I work here. I want to help others, especially young women so that they won't make the same mistakes I did."

"Will you tell me your ideas? I want to help them too," Shawn replied.

The back of her throat felt thick with emotion. For some reason, she felt like Shawn was looking into the depths of her soul. That couldn't be right, could it? He was a businessman, and a very good one if he was already a billionaire at this young age. "What do you want to do with this place? I mean, why come all the way from Chicago to here?"

Shawn ran his tongue over his front teeth. "I asked Lexi the same question. She's my boss. She has connections with so many people and keeps an ear to the ground for places like this that are really striving to make a difference. She understands that they have the possibility to make a huge impact if they get the right funding. That's what Burke's Higher Steps is about."

Carolina rolled her pen back and forth between her fingers. "Well, I'm glad she discovered us."

"Me too," Shawn said. Maybe it was just her imagination, but it seemed like Shawn was saying he was glad he could come to Atlanta to meet her too.

$$\text{❧ } 4 \text{ ☙}$$

Shawn may have crossed a line earlier that day when he asked Carolina about herself, but he didn't regret it. He wanted to get to know her. There was so much in her beautiful mind that intrigued him. He couldn't deny it—he was attracted to Carolina. He found himself looking for her as he walked through the building, continuing to assess the needs of the center. Speaking with her had opened a window into the part of herself that she kept hidden. Once she felt comfortable with him, she'd been vibrant and alive with ideas to help others.

He found Daniel playing with a pile of Legos in a room outside the kitchen.

"Hey, buddy. Cómo estás?" Shawn crouched beside the boy and winked at him.

"Bien," Daniel replied. He handed Shawn a handful of Legos. "Let's build a car."

"Okay. What kind? A racecar?" Shawn sat next to Daniel and began assembling the blocks to resemble a car.

"Maybe. Mommy wants a car someday."

What kind of life did Carolina have, alone and caring for her son by herself? The job at the center was good, but Lisette had shared with him that Carolina volunteered beyond the hours that were allotted to her position. She worked almost full time, but only received part-time wages. "Do you ride the bus?"

Daniel nodded. "We ride the bus, or we walk. Mommy used to ride with me on her bike, but I'm getting too big now."

Shawn pursed his lips as he imagined Carolina, her slight frame, pedaling a bike with a baby seat on the back. Daniel's father must have been a large man, because the boy was tall and solid-looking. "You are a big boy. Do you help your mommy a lot?"

Daniel smiled and nodded his head. "I'm a good boy."

Warmth spread through Shawn's middle. It was apparent that Daniel and Carolina didn't have much, but the love she showed her son was making him into something that no amount of money could buy. Daniel chattered on about cars, bikes, and buses as they built a lopsided racecar and laughed together.

"Why do you dress like that?" Daniel asked, pointing at Shawn's tie. "Are you going to church?"

Shawn chuckled. He looked around the refugee center and noticed the stark difference in his tailored suit and the clothing that the workers and refugees wore. "This is what I usually wear to work, but maybe I should try something different, huh?"

Daniel's lips twitched. "Those aren't work clothes. Those are church clothes."

"Do you go to church with your mommy?"

"Yep. Jesus loves me and my mommy." Daniel grinned and pushed his car across the tile floor.

Shawn watched the little boy play, innocent of the darkness in the world just outside the doors of the center. It had been too many Sundays since Shawn had entered the chapel where he worshipped. He'd put his heart and soul into Burke Enterprises and forgotten about those Sunday hymns he used to sing. With the changes that Jordan Burke had made in his company, Shawn was on track to follow in his footsteps. If he continued on this career path, he'd be a millionaire by the time he was thirty. After that, with his connections and business sense, he'd multiply that until those millions became billions—just like Jordan and Lexi.

Shawn had worked every Sunday for so long that he couldn't remember the last time he'd taken time for God. He sat on the floor surrounded by refugees, people who had given everything for a better, safer life that included worship of their God. His chest filled with warmth. He wanted to be wealthy and successful, but should he pursue money at the loss of his faith?

Shawn studied a family of refugees that Lisette had introduced him to yesterday. She'd explained that they had come from Myanmar—a country that he hardly knew existed before being assigned to this project. It used to be called Burma, and was halfway across the world near Thailand and China, and yet these people had made their way to Atlanta, Georgia, with only the clothes on their backs. With a frown, Shawn stood and walked toward the family. There was something wrong with the world. He couldn't fix it by himself, but with God's help, he could make a difference.

❦   5   ❦

Carolina watched Shawn approach the family from Myanmar, holding her breath. Shawn had been playing with Daniel again—laughing and bringing a smile to her son's face. How could he be so fine-looking and great with kids? And why was she still staring at him? Daniel had mentioned church, and Shawn had been lost in thought for several moments. Carolina carried equipment into the kitchen and even though she told herself not to look, she scanned the room until she saw Shawn. He was watching the other refugees, his forehead drawn with worry.

The head of the family was a man who looked like he was in his forties, but like most of the refugees, he was younger—barely thirty. The stress and conditions that the refugees had to live in aged them. Carolina set the box of supplies on the counter and stood in the doorway of the kitchen. Shawn walked up to the man and gestured at the man's threadbare shirt—so thin that his dark skin showed through the faded material—and then pointed to his blue dress shirt. The man smiled and pointed at his pants, riddled with holes and then at Shawn's dress pants. Shawn chuckled and pulled off his suit coat, hanging it over a chair. Then he removed his tie and hung it over the suit coat. What was he doing? Now she was really in trouble, because his broad shoulders filled out his dress shirt nicely, and she couldn't look away. Shawn began unbuttoning his shirt, and Carolina took a step forward, her heart pushing heat into her face. His fingers moved quickly over the buttons, and before she could ask him what he was doing, he'd removed his shirt and held it out to the man in front of him.

Carolina sucked in a breath. Shawn had some fine shoulders. He wore a thin, white tank top that didn't hide the sculpted muscles of his arms. He turned to pick up his tie, the lines of muscles taut against the fabric.

She should look away, but she couldn't pull her eyes from the man in front of her. He was good looking, but it was his actions that had Carolina riveted to the spot. Shawn held out the fine gray-and-blue tie that matched the shirt, and the man's face lit up with a smile. He pulled on the shirt and carefully buttoned it, the tie hanging loosely around his neck. The refugee smiled and his family reached out their hands, touching Shawn's hands and murmuring in their native language.

Shawn stepped back and picked up his suit coat. He turned slightly as he slipped his bare arms into the jacket, catching Carolina's eye. She was tempted to dash back into the kitchen, but it was obvious she'd been staring at him. Holding up one hand in a wave, Carolina smiled and turned back toward the kitchen.

"Carolina, wait," Shawn said. He hurried toward her, buttoning his suit coat. He grabbed her hand. "Is that okay—what I just did, I mean?"

The part where he showed off his muscled arms, or his tender heart? *I am in trouble.* Carolina's bottom lip trembled, the way it always did when she witnessed charitable acts like Shawn's. "Yes, it was wonderful. Thank you."

"Are you upset?" Shawn's face softened, his eyes full of concern.

Carolina shook her head and leaned toward Shawn, putting her arms around him. He hesitated only a second before he pulled her to him. A thousand thoughts exploded in her head. Why was she hugging Shawn? She hardly knew him, but he had touched her heart in a way that she couldn't ignore. And Shawn didn't seem uncomfortable hugging her. She wanted to stay in his arms, to have him hold her like this, but Carolina pulled back, lifting her head. "That was beautiful. I'm not upset. I just never get used to seeing goodness."

Shawn looked back at the man who moments ago was half-naked and now wore his expensive dress shirt. "I've never done something like that before, but I felt like it was the right thing to do."

"It's more than the shirt. It's the love you gave them." Carolina felt that same love welling up in her heart. Energy arced between her and Shawn, and it was all she could do not to reach out and hug him again.

"Carolina?"

"Yes?"

"Can I take you out to dinner tonight?" He stood there, his bare skin showing above the curve of his tank top underneath his suit coat, and Carolina saw a man who was strong and vulnerable. Wait, did he just ask her out?

"You want to take me on a date?" The hope welling up inside colored her words.

"Yes, but Daniel can come too." Shawn nodded to her sweet boy, still playing with his Lego car. "I'll leave that up to you."

Carolina grinned. Maybe he was asking her just to be nice, or maybe Shawn was too good to be true. Her stomach tightened. Shawn was here on a business trip and would be leaving soon to return to Chicago. She didn't want to be his work fling. Looking down at the floor, she shook her head. "Thanks for the invite, but I want to get Daniel to bed early tonight."

Shawn didn't say anything until Carolina lifted her head. He studied her face, his eyes holding questions that she wished he would ask her. But no, if he asked her more questions, she might end up agreeing to a date. "Are you sure I can't change your mind?"

"Almost," Carolina replied. That was too honest. Why couldn't she have just said, *Yes, I'm sure that I don't want to date a gorgeous man who was considerate enough to think of Daniel when asking me on a date.* Idiot.

"Okay, there's still hope then," Shawn replied, the edge of his mouth quirking up in a grin. "I have to uh—put on another shirt and meet with a few people, but I'll be back at five. Will you have time to go over a few more notes with me?"

Carolina had to bite the inside of her cheek to keep from smiling. They'd gone over all their notes earlier—at least she thought they had. "I'll try to make some time."

Shawn grinned and walked away with purpose. He paused at the doorway and waved at Carolina and she waved back, her heart thumping happily. Why was she smiling and waving at Shawn if she didn't want to go on a date with him? Carolina sighed and returned to her desk. Safety was the most important thing for her and Daniel, but sometimes she wished she had the guts to be a bit more daring.

Carolina worked with Shawn for the better part of the next two days. He was easy to talk to and he listened closely to her ideas.

"I can see why Lisette doesn't ever want you to leave," Shawn said after they'd gone over expense reports and needs for the center.

Carolina's stomach did that little flip like she was inching toward the top of the roller coaster. "I don't want to leave either. This place is like a second home to me."

"You've put your heart into the work, and that's why this center is so successful." Shawn tapped his notebook with a pen. "This assignment has turned out better than I thought it would."

"Oh?" Carolina tilted her head, wondering what he meant. She'd turned him down when he'd asked her out and even though she tried to ignore it, regret had shadowed her the past couple days. If he were to ask her out again, she would definitely say yes.

Shawn met her gaze. "I've really enjoyed getting to know you better. I'm excited to see what Burke's Higher Steps can do to partner with the center."

"Me too. You've been great to work with."

The edges of Shawn's mouth twitched with a smile. "Do you think you might consider going out to dinner with me?"

Carolina was at the top of the roller coaster now, about to take the plunge. If she said yes to Shawn, that would open a door that she had kept firmly shut. She wanted to say yes, even though all of her caution lights were blinking. "I might."

Shawn leaned toward her. "My original invitation still

stands. Daniel is welcome to come along if you'd like. And if I'm making you feel uncomfortable, just say the word and I won't ask again"

Now was the moment for Carolina to decide. She'd kept her heart locked away for so long that she didn't even allow herself to go on casual dates. Over the past week, Shawn had worked with her and given her respect. She still wasn't entirely sure of his aim because he was going back to Chicago, but she was willing to find out. "I think that would be nice."

Shawn's eyes brightened. "Is that a yes?"

Carolina chuckled. "Yes. What time?"

"Does six work?"

Carolina hesitated. "I'll finish work today about five-thirty, but I probably won't get home until after six."

"We could leave from here or I could take you home first if you want to change," Shawn offered.

"Are you sure?" Carolina tried to slow down her thoughts. *Don't get too excited.* It had been months since she'd been on a date, and now this gorgeous, wonderful man wanted to take her, even though he knew she was a single mom.

"Sounds perfect," Carolina said. And maybe it could be. It didn't hurt to have a positive outlook once in a while, did it?

Butterflies. That didn't come close to explaining how Carolina felt as she prepared for her date with Shawn. When Lisette heard what was going on, she had insisted on taking Daniel so that Carolina could have a real date. Shawn had driven her home in his rental car and was waiting outside while she changed into her favorite skirt. It was dark gray with ruffles at the hemline, and she had paired it with a light pink blouse with pearl buttons. It was a great find at the local second-hand store. She looked feminine and beautiful in it. She had a string of fake pearls and dangly silver earrings that she paired with the outfit. Carolina tamed her curly hair, but left it hanging loose over her shoulders. She lifted the fake pearls with her finger. Shawn probably was used to dating women who wore real pearls and had expensive manicures and salon-styled hair. She bit her lower lip. Was she Shawn's version of slumming it while he was visiting Atlanta? Her shoulders tensed as familiar fears and doubts clouded her vision. *Breathe, Carolina.* Shawn had acted completely genuine, so unless she was really off with her man radar or Shawn was an incredible actor, she could relax and give him the ounce of trust needed on this date.

She stepped out of her apartment building and caught sight of Shawn standing outside the passenger door of his car, waiting for her. Oh my, he was fine. Her heart pounded as she reminded herself that this was just a date, nothing more.

"You're beautiful—inside and out," he murmured as he opened the door for her.

"Thank you." Carolina felt heat in her cheeks as she settled into the car. Already blushing and they hadn't even left the parking lot. When Shawn got back in the car, she noticed the fine cut of yet another business suit. This one was paired with a white dress shirt and a dark gray tie, and it fit him perfectly. "You look very nice."

"Thanks. I thought I'd better keep my shirt on for the date." He waggled his eyebrows at her and she giggled.

"Do you ever wear normal clothes?"

"You mean something besides church clothes?" Shawn winked. "That's what Daniel calls my suit."

Carolina smiled. "He's so cute. He loves going to church."

"I noticed that," Shawn said. "It's great to see a kid that young having a relationship with God."

Carolina's heart bumped again. Was Shawn too good to be true? He was gorgeous, giving, and open to her faith. "Is God a part of your life?"

Shawn tapped the steering wheel. "He always has been, but I haven't been doing my part in the relationship lately. I work most Sundays. It's something I want to change."

Hmm, so not a church-goer, but not an atheist either. Carolina noted the word 'change.' How serious was he, though? "I like your honesty, Shawn. It's refreshing."

Shawn turned to her, his eyebrows pulling down in concentration. "That sounds like you haven't always known people who are honest. I'm lucky. Working with the Burkes has taught me a lot."

Carolina looked at her hands clasped in her lap. How much should she share with Shawn?

"I want to get to know you better." Shawn said. "If you're comfortable sharing, I'd love to know what you're thinking right now."

Warmth flooded her middle. He was speaking the truth—not trying to flatter her into a one-night stand. She breathed in and out, reminding herself that she didn't have to repeat the past. Carolina closed her eyes for half a second. "Well, I made a lot of bad choices when

I first came to America, and a lot of that had to do with how young I was. People took advantage of me. The man who was Daniel's father. He wanted me to get an abortion." Carolina closed her eyes, holding her breath.

Eddie was her whole world, and she fell madly in love with him. She thought he might marry her when he found out she was pregnant, but she had been wrong. So wrong. Eddie took her to an abortion clinic and dropped her off. She had protested the entire way there until Eddie smacked her and told her not to come back to him until the problem was resolved. She had walked away from the abortion clinic that day and away from Eddie and the imagined love he had given her.

"He sounds despicable. I wouldn't use the word 'father' to describe him," Shawn said.

Carolina raised her head. "You're right. He's never been a father to Daniel. He has nothing to do with him and that's how I want it to be. Sometimes my heart hurts for Daniel, and I wish I had made better choices." Carolina took a deep breath.

Shawn reached over and took her hand, giving it a gentle squeeze. "I admire you. You're a strong woman."

With Shawn holding her hand, Carolina's heart beat so loud she worried he might hear it. His touch sent heat through her skin, and she didn't want him to let go. *But what does my heart know?* It was hard to let herself fall into the moment, knowing how her heart had betrayed her before. "I want to do the right thing for Daniel. I'm only twenty-one, and I know I can't rely on the center forever, but I love working there."

Shawn moved his thumb back and forth over her hand. "I don't see why you couldn't continue working at the center. Lisette has nothing but good to say about you."

"Thank you," Carolina said. "But we rely on donations, and every year there are new laws and rules based on what kind of funding we can get from the government. I just think it's smart for me to look ahead to what other options I have to take care of my son."

"Well, you're definitely bright enough that you could go to college. Have you considered taking some online classes?"

He thought she was bright? Carolina pushed her palm closer to his, feeling the heat of his hand against hers. It was warm, just like the compliments he'd given her. Shawn seemed sincere, and Carolina wanted to believe his words. "I thought I would wait until Daniel was in school. I want to give him attention when we're at home, because when I'm at work he has to rely on a lot of different people for his care."

"I understand. You're a good person, Carolina. If the world could have a dose of your unselfishness, things would be a lot different."

His words felt like a soft blanket wrapped around her shoulders. She was safe for the moment. Carolina let her fears subside. What if Shawn Halstrom really was as good as he seemed? What if he didn't have to leave in two weeks to go back to Chicago? She could daydream for a moment. They continued to talk as they drove until they reached a restaurant on the other side of town. Carolina hardly ever got to eat out, and especially not at a fancy restaurant. The neon sign said The Piano Guy, and Shawn explained that he was taking her to a piano bar, basically a karaoke bar featuring people who played the piano.

"I hope you like it. I've only been once before. When I was looking up suggestions, this popped up and I didn't want to miss it."

"I love music," Carolina said.

"Me too." Shawn took her hand again as they walked into the restaurant and waited to be seated. "And good food. This place is supposed to be great."

Jazzy piano music filtered through the air from the grand piano in the corner of the room. Several people talked and laughed near the beautiful instrument. A young black man played, his fingers traveling along the keys at lightning speed. Carolina tapped her foot to the beat and smiled at Shawn. "This'll be fun."

"It might be more fun if I played the piano and could impress my date," Shawn said.

Carolina leaned closer to him and whispered in his ear. "You don't have to play the piano to impress me. I saw a piece of your heart the day you gave your shirt to that man. It reminded me that there are good men in the world."

Shawn turned his head. His face was only a breath away from hers. His eyes flicked to her lips, and then he put his arm around her. "I'm glad you think so. I'm going to try to find more pieces of my heart to give."

Once they were seated and had placed their orders, Carolina and Shawn sat together listening and commenting on the different music. A guy with curly red hair played a haunting melody and then a blues rendition, and then a young Latina woman played a classical piece. Everyone seemed to be having a good time. Shawn seemed so aware of her, and she couldn't seem to get her heart rate under control all evening. He touched her arm and leaned in close to speak with her when the music got louder. His beard tickled her face, and Carolina was tempted to reach out and touch it, to touch him.

The server brought out crab and pasta with various sauces, and Carolina ate until her stomach was full. Even all these years later, that feeling was unfamiliar to her. Hunger had been a constant companion through most of her life.

"So how do you like the food?" Shawn asked pointing his fork at her plate. "Looks like you could eat more."

Carolina chuckled. "If I take another bite, I might explode. But this is absolutely delicious. Thank you." She pushed the noodles into a pile. "It still seems weird to me not to be hungry every day." She looked absently around the room. "I'd never seen so much food until I came to America."

Shawn tilted his head, an expression of sympathy tightening his eyes. "I can't imagine what that must have been like. You have so much to offer people. We need reminders of how blessed our lives are."

"I agree," Carolina said. "That's part of the reason I'm so invested in the center. All the wealth and abundance sometimes derails a person. When refugees arrive, there's so much. They don't know how to handle it all." Carolina leaned forward. "That's why I want to get these trainings in place. Help them understand finances, education, and how to keep their family strong in a different world."

Shawn reached for her hand again and squeezed it. "I want you to know that I'm very impressed with what I've seen at the Heart of Atlanta Center. I can't wait to share my intel with Burke's Higher Steps."

Carolina's eyes brimmed with tears. She swept them away before they could drop from her lashes. "Thank you, Shawn. It must feel so good to be able to make such a difference."

"It does, but this is the foundation, not me. I want to do more, though."

The server came in and offered them dessert. While Shawn ordered chocolate molten cake, Carolina thought about his comments. She thought Shawn was a billionaire and that he was funding the donation from Burke's

Higher Steps, but he had just said the foundation was the one giving the donation. Maybe she had misunderstood his place in the company. Carolina shrugged inwardly; Shawn hadn't acted any different toward her, even though he was obviously wealthy. Whether he was a billionaire or not, Carolina's heart was entangled in his.

$$\text{\ding{167}} \quad 7 \quad \text{\ding{168}}$$

It was nine o'clock by the time Shawn left the piano bar with Carolina. Man, he didn't want the night to end. He bit back the desire he felt every time he looked at her. Carolina had to be aware of the effect she was having on him. She'd opened up to him more, but was it wishful thinking on his part that she might be interested in him?

They stopped by Lisette's house to pick up a sleepy Daniel, and Shawn carried him carefully to the car. When they were on their way again, Carolina put her hand over his. "You must have a big family. You're a natural with kids."

Shawn coughed. The thought of him being a natural with kids was the opposite of his fears. "You really think so?"

"Sure," Carolina responded. "Daniel was even talking about you yesterday."

Shawn grinned. "Truthfully, I haven't spent much time around kids. I have two younger brothers, but none of us have settled down yet."

"Is that something you want to do? Settle down, I mean."

Shawn felt the heat from Carolina's hand on his, and he turned his palm over, interlacing their fingers. "I do. At first, I wasn't sure how it was possible with how much I work, but lately I've had a change of heart. My boss, Lexi Burke, and her brother Jordan have both made some pretty radical changes in their life, and they seem very happy." Shawn took in a breath, concentrating on Carolina's tender skin under his fingertips. "You?"

She looked over at him, biting her lower lip. "Family is very important to me. I don't know if I'll get a chance to right the wrongs I've made, but I do hope for more in my future."

"For a church-going girl, you sure are missing the messages," Shawn said. "Our God is a forgiving God. You've fixed things with Him, right?"

Carolina nodded.

"Then your wrongs are gone unless you repeat them again."

"Do you really believe that?" she whispered. "I want to believe it, I do, but there's a part of me that feels broken."

Shawn pulled in front of her rundown apartment and put the car in park. Normally he avoided parking in risky areas like this apartment building. It hit him with a jolt, just how far removed he was from Carolina's lifestyle—how little he understood about her struggle to provide for her son. He leaned over and put his arm around Carolina, pulling her close. "You aren't broken. I've never met someone with a heart as strong as yours." He touched her face and leaned closer. He wanted to kiss her like nothing he'd ever wanted before, but he held back. Carolina had been taken advantage of by a man who was only interested in her body. In only a few days, she had shown Shawn that her spirit was bright, vibrant, and beautiful. He smiled and leaned back. "I'd better help you get that little boy to bed."

Carolina held his gaze, a look of longing in her dark eyes, but then she gave her head a little shake and got out of the car before Shawn could get her door. He helped her carry Daniel up two flights of stairs. "I can get him from here." Carolina held out her arms.

She didn't want him to see her apartment, because she was embarrassed by her circumstances, but he held Daniel tightly. "Carolina, let me help you. Please."

Her shoulders slumped, and she unlocked the flimsy front door, opening it slowly. *I won't let on how I feel about her home.* He surveyed her apartment, keeping his mask in place. It was neat and clean. There was a sense of love and home. He carried Daniel to the one bedroom and peeked inside. There were two twin beds in the room. The floor was littered with cars and blocks, but the beds were tidy, and the plastic dresser had a picture of Carolina holding her son and smiling brightly.

She pulled back the covers of the bed decorated with a patchwork quilt, and Shawn carefully set the sleeping boy down, adjusting the pillow. He followed Carolina out of the bedroom and into the living room that was open to the kitchen. "Your apartment feels like a home. It's really nice," he said.

Carolina looked down at her feet. "Thank you."

"Hey." Shawn stepped forward and put a finger under her chin, lifting her beautiful eyes to his. "I mean it."

Carolina folded her arms around her middle and shook her head. "We're two steps away from poverty. I know that."

Her words were like a knife to Shawn's heart. Flashes of his life in Chicago buzzed through his mind. His penthouse apartment with two bedrooms and an office—all for one person. He'd been living life oblivious to the real world around him. He could probably help Carolina, but he didn't want her to feel ashamed. What could he say to her? He pulled a breath in through his nose.

"You have taken what you have and made it beautiful. You're an excellent mother, and you love your son. That is far from poverty, if you ask me."

Carolina lifted her head and gave him a tentative

smile. "You're right. I am very blessed. I was worried what you might think because…"

"I don't care where you live. I want to know you," Shawn said. "Will you give me a chance?"

"But what chance do we really have?" Carolina asked. "Aren't you leaving next week?"

Shawn rubbed a hand over his beard. "Yes, but I'll be back." Lexi had asked him to stay as long as necessary to figure out what the center needed. If he didn't have pressing work in Chicago, he would have extended his trip. He didn't want to leave Carolina. "I thought I could get the job done quickly and get back to Chicago, but I've had a change of heart, and that means I need to do a little more work here."

He took a step closer to her, inhaling the sweet scent of her perfume. He dipped his head and brushed a kiss over her lips. Carolina responded, kissing him back and putting her arms around his waist. He kissed her once more, and then held her close, feeling the warmth of her body against his. "I'd better go." His voice was husky, and Carolina nodded against his chest.

"Thank you for tonight," she said.

"Can I pick you up tomorrow morning?"

"We usually catch the eight o'clock bus."

"Then I'll be here at eight-thirty." He touched her cheek. "Sweet dreams."

"See you tomorrow."

Shawn used every ounce of his willpower to walk out the door of her apartment and down the filthy staircase. His phone pinged as he was getting in the car. Lexi texted him asking how things were going. Shawn sent a quick reply, letting her know that he was planning to return to Atlanta after he finished with work at headquarters. He would need at least another week to research the needs of the facility and the crazy thumping of his heart whenever he thought of the beautiful Carolina. Lexi would be thrilled to hear the other motivation behind his extended stay, but he wasn't about to disclose the matters of his heart yet.

Was that because he really didn't know his heart yet, or was he afraid of what Lexi might say? As he drove back to his hotel, a flicker of doubt crowded out the memory of kissing Carolina. She had warmed to him rather quickly for being so hesitant at first. What if Carolina's motivation had more to do with money than him? He grimaced. This wasn't how he wanted to spend his drive, but once the thought surfaced, it continued circling. Women always loved his money and image; why did he believe that Carolina would be any different?

And while he was on Worry Street, he might as well acknowledge that his parents would likely find the idea of his dating a Cuban refugee a departure from common sense. His dad would use the gold-digger card, and his mother probably wouldn't even take him seriously. Shawn rolled his shoulders back and refocused on the great evening he'd shared with Carolina. It was too early to be worrying like this. He found his way back to his hotel and relived the kiss once more with a smile. It was too early to worry, and definitely too early to regret kissing her.

$\maltese$ 8 $\maltese$

The sun seemed to shine brighter the next day when Carolina awoke to Daniel crawling in bed with her. He made motor noises for the truck he was driving. Carolina allowed herself to lie in bed for a few extra minutes, thinking about Shawn. Her stomach fluttered with anticipation of the day ahead. She had met a man who was kind and good, and he wanted to know her. That thought pulled her from the soft confines of her bed and moved her into action.

"Daniel, let's get ready for the day," Carolina said.

"I don't want to go to work today," Daniel pouted.

This was a common complaint from Daniel, at least in the past few months. He was growing older and getting tired of spending the long hours at the center. "Guess what? Shawn is going to pick us up today so we don't have to ride the bus."

Daniel jumped up, grinning. "I'm ready to go now!"

Carolina laughed. "Let's have breakfast first and tidy up. Then we can go with Shawn."

Daniel chattered happily as she poured him a bowl of cornflakes and sliced a few strawberries on top. Carolina let her mind wander to the possibility of how life might be if she were to marry someone—someone like Shawn. She wanted that more than she ever admitted because it was too painful for her heart. But while they ate breakfast in their tiny apartment that smelled faintly of mildew, Carolina thought about how much she wanted to be loved by a man who could take care of her and her son. Her dreams didn't have a lot to do with great wealth, huge houses, and fancy cars. She was happy with the simple life, just knowing that she could stay in one place and be secure.

Who am I kidding? Shawn would be leaving Atlanta next week, and even though he said he'd be back, it wasn't a sure thing. She was nothing more than a diversion during his business trip. Sure, they'd connected, but to honestly think she had a chance with someone of his status was more than wishful thinking. It was ridiculous. She touched up her lipstick in the mirror, and the reflection of a single mother near poverty drained her lovesick feelings immediately. *Get your stuff together, Carolina, and quit letting the beat of your heart lead you astray.*

Shawn knocked on the door at 8:25, and Daniel squealed with delight. When Carolina opened the door,

Daniel launched himself at Shawn's legs, hugging him tightly. "You're here! Can I ride in your car?"

Shawn hugged Daniel and looked at Carolina, his eyes lit up with a joy she hadn't noticed before. Her pep talk from earlier vaporized. "Hey, buddy, you rode in my car last night, but you don't remember it."

Daniel put a hand to his head and closed his eyes. "Nope. Don't remember."

Shawn chuckled and rubbed a hand over Daniel's thick black hair.

He leaned in and kissed Carolina's cheek in a movement that surprised her. She could get used to that, and his manly smell was irresistible. She reached up and touched his face, her fingers trailing along the edge of his beard. "It's good to see you this morning."

Shawn looked at her and Daniel with such tenderness that her heart felt warm and gooey, like a hot chocolate chip cookie fresh out of the oven. He took her hand and held Daniel's with the other, and they walked out of the apartment building together. Carolina left her doubts on the doorstep. So what if Shawn was only around for two weeks? It didn't mean that Carolina couldn't get to know him. And more kissing would definitely be a good thing. She smiled and tamed her thoughts, shifting gears into working mode so that she could think over the warmth spreading from her middle to the tips of her fingers. On the ride over, they discussed what needed to be done that day at the center.

"Last night I found some sites that can order materials needed from the countries of the refugees." She didn't tell him that she'd done the research when she couldn't sleep last night because of the tingling in her lips. "And there was another site with a lot of great materials that I think they could work with also."

"That'll be great. I'm thinking of another idea I wanted to talk to you about," Shawn said. "Have you thought about building a playground outside the center?"

Carolina sat up straighter in her seat. "That's been a dream of mine from the very beginning. There's not much for the little kids to do." She sighed. "But the problem is that empty lot next to us hasn't been available. When we checked a couple years ago, the person who owned it was thinking of building a business. I'm not sure what's happened since then."

"Well, I can definitely find out." Shawn reached over and took Carolina's hand. She didn't think she could get used to the way it felt to have this man hold her hand gently and look at her with appreciation in his eyes. When they arrived at the refugee center, Shawn met with Lisette while Carolina worked through the regular tasks that couldn't wait. At lunch time, they met up in the cafeteria and enjoyed a bowl of gumbo, with Shawn commenting on Southern food and how the rest of the world was missing out.

"So let's brainstorm this playground idea," Shawn said. "Are you any good at sketching?"

Carolina shrugged. "I could give it a try." She grabbed a sheet of paper and pencil and sketched out the area next to the Heart of Atlanta Center. Swings, a teeter-totter, and monkey bars would make quite a difference in some of these kids' lives. That little bit of activity would brighten their day. While she sketched out the playground ideas and listed the equipment they would need, Shawn scrolled through a website on his phone for playground equipment costs. He jotted down costs and began writing up a proposal to take to the planning and zoning committee of the city. "I think we should move on this before something happens to that empty lot over there."

"Okay, it's worth a try," Carolina said. She felt a surge of creative energy with Shawn encouraging her dreams. There were so many possibilities to help people through the center, but most of the ideas Carolina had were tucked away, seemingly too impossible to even dream about. Now Shawn had opened the door to those locked-up dreams, and Carolina felt like the whole world lay at her feet.

❧ 9 ☙

Shawn worked with Carolina for two hours, going over plans and ideas before he had to leave to meet with the city zoning committee about the possibility of expanding the center and adding a playground. The morning was gone before he realized it, and Shawn didn't want to leave her side. His heart thumped happily when she smiled at him and touched his hand before he left. He wanted to keep that smile on her face.

Shawn drove downtown and met with the director of the planning and zoning committee for the city. Max Lawson was a no-nonsense businessman, and after speaking with him for a few minutes, Shawn learned that Max had started his own chain of restaurants and retired, only to step back into working for the city.

"I don't see anything wrong with these plans, son,"

Max pointed at the proposal sheet Shawn had prepared. "But there is a problem with your location."

"What do you mean?" Shawn asked.

"The city has been looking for new areas to build schools, and your center is part of one of our top choices. We are thinking about buying up that property and helping the center relocate."

Shawn let his business mask slip into place, not allowing his emotions to show. "Is that the best decision for the center? I was under the impression that location is ideal for the refugees as they are transitioning into society. The bus routes run to and from the center with plenty of cheap housing along the way, and there's a great community of Hispanics that many of the refugees from Cuba are able to take part in."

Max waved his hand and shook his head. "It doesn't really matter. They can transition somewhere else."

"Is this plan final or still in the works?"

Max grinned. "We've still got a ways to go. We're in the planning stages and still scoping out areas. But this one will probably be the winner because the center is leasing it from the city." He handed the paperwork back to Shawn. "Why don't you work up a few more details on your proposal and resubmit it. That should give us enough time to make a final decision. We'll be ready to move ahead in the next couple months."

Shawn swallowed. He wasn't planning to be in Atlanta

two months from now, but what Max had revealed could mean the end of the Heart of Atlanta Refugee Center. "If it's all the same to you, I'd like to submit this proposal now, and we'll continue working on more details. I'm not going to be in town for too long."

Max hesitated, his brow furrowed. "Okay, I'll get that submitted for you."

Shawn's stomach twisted as an uneasy feeling came over him. He thought about pushing the issue, but in the end walked away with Max holding a copy of the proposal in his hands. If he were a betting man, he'd put odds that those papers would never be filed. Shawn left the office with a new resolve. He dialed Lexi's cell number as he pulled back onto the street.

"Shawn, how are things going down there? Isn't that center amazing?" Lexi's cheerful voice landed hard on Shawn's heart.

"It is, but I'm afraid we have a problem." Shawn explained his encounter with Max Lawson to Lexi, telling her his fears that the center would have to be relocated.

"What?! They can't do that. We need to find out if the city really owns the center and if there are outstanding loans on the mortgage. You've done good work, Shawn. We have to make this right."

"You can count on me." Shawn ended the call. He knew what Lexi wanted, and he knew what needed to be done. He drove down the street, but wasn't ready to return to the refugee center yet. He pulled his car off the road and dialed the lawyer on staff for Burke Enterprises. Thirty minutes later, Shawn had a plan. Unfortunately, that plan meant he needed to high-tail it back to Chicago that night.

❧ 10 ☙

Carolina tried to focus on her computer screen, but the twisting in her gut made it impossible. Shawn had disappeared, just like that. He'd called her two hours ago as he was rushing to the airport. He said that he had urgent business that was taking him back to Chicago, but a part of her was afraid that he had found a way for a quick escape without sticky goodbyes and taken it.

"Hello in there," Lisette called as she walked through the office and up to Carolina's desk.

"What? Oh, hi," Carolina answered, straightening and refocusing on her computer.

"Something's worrying you, and I'm guessing it has to do with a handsome man who is leaving town."

Leave it to Lisette to get straight to the heart of the matter. Carolina sighed. "I shouldn't have gone on a date with him, or ridden to and from work with him, or kissed him."

"You kissed him? Girl, you've been holding out on me." Lisette put a hand on her hip. "I don't understand why you would regret spending time with Shawn. He's a great guy."

Carolina shook her head. "I think I was probably just a work fling. He didn't even have to say goodbye—well, except over the phone."

"He's coming back."

"How do you know?" Carolina asked, hope flaring in her question. If he did come back, would she be able to give him more of her heart than he'd already taken?

Lisette leaned forward and tapped Carolina's phone. "He called me and told me he's coming back, just like he told you." She grinned and shook her head. "For such a smart girl, you sure are missing the clues."

"Clues to what?"

"Shawn likes you. He called you before he got on the plane. If he really wanted to skip town, he wouldn't have done that. He's coming back, and you'll still be working together. Don't write him off because you're scared."

Carolina gripped the edge of the desk. "But I am scared." And her heart was clay in Shawn's hands right then. She wished she hadn't given him any control over her heart, while at the same time, she couldn't wait to see him again.

Lisette patted Carolina's back. "He'll be gone for a

week. Let the dust settle, and see how your heart feels when he comes back."

"I guess I can do that." Carolina pursed her lips and squinted at her computer screen, not really focusing on anything.

"Sure you can. What other choice do you have?" Lisette said. She smiled and left the room, her question tapping on the edges of Carolina's heart.

❧ 11 ❧

The return flight to Atlanta felt twice as long as it had the first time Shawn had made the trip. Over the past week, he'd called and texted Carolina every day. She'd seemed somewhat distant and hesitant, and Shawn hated being apart from her. He'd worked twelve hour days to get everything done at Burke Enterprises and plans had been put into motion to potentially change the fate of the refugee center in a miraculous way *if* everything turned out as he hoped.

He drove from the airport straight to the Heart of Atlanta Center, his smile broadening with every mile he crossed. Things were still new and fragile with Carolina, but his feelings hadn't evaporated when he left her presence. If anything, his desire for her—to know her and Daniel—was stronger.

He parked the rental car and hurried into the center

looking for Carolina. Lisette was in her office on the phone, so Shawn waved and tried to walk nonchalantly down the hall toward Carolina's work space. The beating of his heart could not be described as nonchalant as he turned the corner and caught sight of dark black curls. Carolina leaned forward, studying something on her computer screen.

"Hey, beautiful," Shawn said.

Carolina jerked back in her chair, her hand covering her heart. "Shawn, you startled me." She glanced at her watch. "You got in early?"

Shawn grinned. "I might have driven a little faster than the posted speed limit." He walked toward her and took her hand, squeezing her fingertips. "I missed you."

Carolina smiled, but carefully removed her hand from his. "Lisette is going to be so happy you're back. We've been working nonstop on filling in every detail of the assessment you sent us."

Ouch. Carolina had totally brushed him off. He opened his mouth, but the right words didn't come, so he closed it and cleared his throat. "That's good to hear. I waved at Lisette on my way in. How is Daniel today?"

"He's at a friend's house for a few hours. A rare treat." Her smile was tight. "I'm just going to finish up this analysis, and then I can help you with whatever you need, okay?"

Shawn took a step back, as if Carolina's words had physically pushed him out of her space. "Carolina, I—"

"There you are," Lisette said as she entered the room. "I should have known I would find you here. Have you two had a chance to visit?" Her smile hinted at a meaning deeper than her words.

"Actually, I was just about—"

"Yes, Shawn was just leaving so that I can finish up with this report," Carolina replied. She looked at Lisette, but avoided his eyes. "I have to hurry so that I can go pick up Daniel."

What was happening? Shawn looked down at his hands, wondering if they would fade into a mist—part of some nightmarish dream world he'd stepped into. He tried to slip his business mask into place, but it caught somewhere above his eyebrows, leaving him exposed.

He nodded toward Lisette. "I have a lot to go over with you, but let me know if you'd rather start tomorrow."

Lisette looked at him and then Carolina with a furrowed brow. "I have some time now. Let's see what we can get done. And Carolina?"

Carolina looked up as Shawn moved to stand beside Lisette. "Yes?"

"I'll need you to go over everything with Shawn tomorrow so we can hit the ground running."

"Okay. I can do that." Her voice was emotionless, but at the last second, Carolina's eyes flicked to Shawn's, and it felt like he was looking in a mirror at his own hurt. She hunched over her computer screen, breaking eye contact again. Shawn walked slowly out with Lisette, wondering what had just happened. After he sat down in Lisette's office, he patted the pockets of his suit jacket, feeling like he'd forgotten something. He had his wallet and cell phone. It took him a few seconds to realize what was missing. His heart was sitting on Carolina's desk, and he didn't know how to get it back.

❧ 12 ❧

Carolina slipped out of the center forty minutes later and walked five blocks to pick up Daniel from his friend's house. No matter how many times she swallowed, she couldn't get rid of the metallic taste in her mouth. It tasted like hurt, and it looked like Shawn's eyes. She had been a master at concealing her emotions and delivered the death blow to their budding relationship just as she'd practiced. Shawn was ever the gentleman and didn't push her—he was probably too confused to know how to react. Everything was going fine until Carolina had made the mistake of looking into his eyes. The pain throbbed. It was the same pain throbbing in her own heart as it cried out for her to stop and give him a chance. But she didn't stop, and she couldn't give him a chance, because when everything was over, he would still return to Chicago.

It was better to feel some pain now and keep her distance until everything was resolved. Shawn Halstrom would be gone soon, and her heart would recover. Hopefully.

◈

Carolina called in sick the next day, thinking that a little more distance from Shawn's blue eyes might cure her heartache. She spent the day cleaning her apartment and playing with Daniel.

"Mommy, I want to play trucks." Daniel pushed the cars and trucks that Shawn had given him over the carpet.

"Okay, where should we drive?" Carolina knelt down and pushed one of the cars around a stain on the carpet that had been there when they moved in.

"Let's drive to Shawn's house. He likes cars." Daniel made motor noises as he pushed his car alongside Carolina's. "I like Shawn."

He said it matter-of-factly, with such certainty that he would see Shawn again. Carolina bit her lip. Maybe she'd done the wrong thing in pushing Shawn away.

A knock sounded on her door, and Carolina's breath caught in her throat. She'd paid all of her bills, and she wasn't late on rent. Ticking off the items in her mind reassured her that all was well. She thought that until she looked in the peephole and saw who had knocked on her door. Shawn.

The doorknob was cool to her touch, and Carolina hesitated a second. Maybe he came to say goodbye. *Maybe that's what I should say. Yes.* She nodded. *I'll open the door and tell him goodbye.* She turned the doorknob. Maybe Shawn would return her heart while he was at it.

With a tug, she pulled the door open halfway. "I missed you today. I brought something to help you feel better." Shawn smiled and stepped forward, holding out a dozen red roses and a grocery sack. "Can I talk to you for a minute? I brought something for Daniel too."

"Shawn!" Daniel ran around Carolina and hugged Shawn's legs.

"Hey, buddy! How are you? I missed you too. How are your cars and trucks driving?"

"Me and Mommy are driving. You want to play?" Daniel tugged on Shawn's arm.

Now she would have to let him in. "Please, come in."

He handed her the flowers, but held tight to the grocery sack. "How are you feeling?"

"These flowers are beautiful." *And so are you.* Carolina tried to calm her traitorous heart that Shawn obviously had brought with him, because her chest came alive as soon as he smiled at her. "You shouldn't have come by, though. I'll be back to work tomorrow."

"Hey, Daniel, do you want to get the cars set up, and

I'll come drive with you after I talk to your mom?" Daniel yipped and ran into the bedroom.

Shawn set the grocery sack on the counter and stepped toward Carolina. "Please," he whispered, "tell me what I did wrong so that I can fix it."

She shook her head. "There's nothing wrong. I just didn't feel good." The lie fell flat, and Shawn tilted his head as if he had her plugged into a lie-detection test.

"You were avoiding me today. Stop it." He took her hand, but didn't let go when she pulled back. "Carolina. I came back, and I'm not leaving without a chance to take you on another date."

Her fingers tingled every place his skin touched hers. "And what if I say no?" *Because I'm scared stupid, and I can't stop thinking about kissing you again.* Carolina sucked in a breath, afraid she'd spoken her thoughts aloud. Shawn's lips twitched, and he shook his head.

"If you said no, I would honor you even though you're a terrible liar. What are you afraid of?" He squeezed her hand, sending another jolt of pleasant thrills along her arm.

"You came back, but you're leaving again." Carolina tugged on her hand, and this time he let go.

"And what if I came back again? Will you fake sick again?" He waved a hand around her tiny apartment. "This place looks pretty clean for a sick person's house."

She rolled her eyes, at the same time feeling a surge

of happiness that he had noticed her efforts to clean that day. "The point is you'll eventually leave. For good."

"No, that's not true. Last month, I would have agreed with you, but things change." Shawn lifted his hand and tucked a strand of hair behind her ear. "Things are changing with my job, and I've had some different options open up. I'm going to be in Atlanta for several weeks, and I want to spend time with you and Daniel."

Her resistance engine clunked to a stop. "Wait. Do you really mean it?"

"Yeah, and I even brought dinner with me. It's the perfect thing for someone who is 'sick.'" He did air quotes with his fingers and smirked at her.

Carolina laughed. She had been sick—at heart. But just having Shawn here and talking to her made her feel like maybe she could trust the chance life was giving her. "I really have been sick."

"Yeah, me too." Shawn put his hand over his heart. He winked and walked over to the grocery sack and unloaded several Styrofoam containers of food. "I bought chicken noodle soup and whole wheat bread."

He pulled a loaf of bread out of the sack, and Carolina's mouth watered. "That smells delicious."

"My mother always made this for me and my brothers when we got sick."

Carolina pulled out bowls and spoons so they could dish up the comfort food.

"I'm ready to play," Daniel said. He had been lingering in the doorway of the bedroom, and now he had his cars and trucks set up on the kitchen floor.

"Okay, let's play for a few minutes, if it's okay with your mom." Shawn looked toward Carolina, and she nodded.

With a grin, Shawn patted Daniel's head, and then turned the full wattage of his smile on Carolina. "Just one more thing I need to do first, little buddy." He walked over and pulled her in close to his chest.

"Oh," Carolina said, but she didn't push him away. He smelled like sea salt and spice mixed with the warm bread wafting through the kitchen. She looked at his lips, remembering the kisses that they'd shared.

Shawn tipped her chin up and kissed her full on the mouth. Carolina wrapped her arms around his neck and kissed him in return as all of her plans to keep her heart safe melted into a puddle at her feet.

Shawn pulled back, and then kissed the sides of her mouth, his lips tilting up in a smile. "Thank you," he whispered. He gave her a hug, and then released her with whoop as he chased Daniel around the cramped kitchen with his cars.

Carolina leaned back against the counter, listening for warning signs, but all she felt was the thump-thump of her heart. She felt warm and safe there for the moment. Carolina watched Shawn play with Daniel, and kicked the fear out of her mind. Shawn was trying to show how much he cared for her and Daniel. Even though the future was uncertain, Carolina decided she was going to give him a chance.

❧ 13 ☙

"Hey, Earth to Carolina!" Lisette called.

Carolina jumped and banged her knee against her computer desk. "Ouch!"

"Sorry, I tried to get through the Shawn daydream, but you must have been in deep," Lisette replied with a laugh.

"Yeah, I won't try to deny it," Carolina responded. Her fingers went to her lips, thinking of the kisses that Shawn had given her that morning when he picked her up for work. Shawn had returned to Atlanta a little over two weeks ago, and every day, Carolina was falling harder for him.

"Your head is in the clouds in a good way, girl," Lisette said.

Carolina ducked her head, blushing. She had been thinking about Shawn. She thought about him every

73

spare minute, and was finding it hard to concentrate on her work. Lisette was the one who wanted them to work together, though, so she could take part of the blame. But that thought made Carolina jerk her head up and narrow her eyes. "This is all your doing, you know."

Lisette tapped her head. "This brain of mine works overtime helping make lives better." She winked. "Now what do you think of Shawn?"

Carolina didn't try to hide her smile. "I think I may be in trouble, or at least my heart is in trouble." She and Shawn had worked together and seen each other every day since he'd returned. He picked her and Daniel up every morning and drove them to the center, and had taken them out to dinner several times, returning them to the apartment afterwards. He always kept the good night kisses brief and left her wanting more. "Do you think I'm crazy to think I have a chance with someone like him?"

Lisette stood next to Carolina's desk and put her hand on her shoulder. "I think Shawn's asking the same questions."

Carolina shook her head. "No, he isn't."

"Yes, he is. To me." Lisette came around the desk and pulled up a chair. "He asked me if I thought he had a chance with someone like you, because he has so little experience with kids. But I can tell you that he loves Daniel."

"I know. I think that's what scares me. I can't find anything wrong with him."

"Haven't you ever heard that you aren't supposed to borrow trouble?" Lisette asked. "He is a good man. He wants to do good things in the world, and he could change your life."

Lisette spoke the very words that Carolina had thought. Those same words seemed to condemn her, because she was not a gold digger, but she also wasn't blind to the possibilities that Shawn could open in her life. He was educated, with so many resources at his fingertips. Carolina worried every month about how she would make ends meet if ever an emergency arose. She had barely enough money to pay her rent and buy groceries with government assistance. Now that she knew Shawn and the foundation he was involved with, Burke's Higher Steps, Carolina felt confident that if she ever fell on hard times, she would have an alternative. Through hard work and good connections, she and Daniel would be safe.

"You could do a lot worse than date Shawn Halstrom. I know you're young and you made a bad choice, but those are behind you, Carolina." Lisette patted her knee. "Life can be good. It can be better than we've ever dreamed about."

"Thanks, Lisette. I hope you're right."

❧ 14 ❧

"I want to take you for a drive this Saturday," Shawn said during his fourth week back in Atlanta. They were at her apartment enjoying Chinese takeout, which was a great reward after all the work they'd accomplished. Carolina's mind was still spinning through ideas of the playground and how it would improve the center. "I want you to show me some parts of Atlanta and the surrounding area that I haven't seen."

Carolina swallowed hard. How could she explain to Shawn that she'd hardly ever ventured outside of the city? She'd only gone as far as public transit could take her; her life was filled with work and mothering Daniel, not sightseeing.

"What's wrong?" Shawn asked.

Carolina pressed her teeth against her bottom lip,

still trying to think of how to answer him. Her life was pathetic compared to his.

"You know, when you do that, it makes me want to kiss you," Shawn murmured. Carolina laughed. When she was with Shawn, she forgot about her life status, and that was a good thing. She leaned over and kissed Shawn's cheek just above the line of his beard. She felt the whiskers against her cheek as he grabbed her and kissed her on the mouth. Carolina giggled again, falling back into his arms on the couch. Shawn stroked her hair, his fingers catching in her curls. "Tell me what's in that pretty head of yours."

"The truth is, I haven't really seen Atlanta or the state of Georgia. I've only survived here."

Shawn was quiet, nodding his head slowly. "I'm sorry. How do you do it? You're not bitter or resentful. You're happy." He leaned forward and kissed her cheek. "You have a glow about you."

Carolina snuggled back into his chest, enjoying the feel of his strong arms wrapped around her. Daniel sat at their feet, eating a package of gummies, happily munching away, unaware of anything but his treat. "I live this way because I remember Cuba," Carolina said. "I tell myself to never forget. The danger. The fear. The hunger. I never want to forget how much I have now."

"I haven't wanted to say anything before, Carolina, but I have to say it now." Shawn turned to face her. "I never want you to have that fear again. No matter what happens. I don't want you to worry that your rent will be paid. Your job at the center will be secure. You can depend on that."

"What are you saying?" Carolina's heart tripped with fear. Was Shawn hinting at goodbye? Had she really been dreaming of grand visions of a life with him that weren't possible?

"I'm saying that I care for you and hope you feel the same, but even if you don't, you'll still have your job at the center."

Carolina felt the back of her throat burn with emotion. He *was* saying goodbye, and he was telling her not to worry about her job. In a sense, he was paying her off so that he didn't feel guilty about leaving. "You don't have to give me special treatment. If the center needs to make budget cuts, I can find another job. I knew you were leaving when we went on our first date. It's okay. I understand."

"No, you don't understand." Shawn shook his head. He blinked, and there was uncertainty behind his eyes. He blew out a breath and blinked slowly. "That didn't come out right. I'm trying to say that I care about you. I don't know what will happen with my next assignment, but right now, I want to be with you."

She shook her head, not letting herself believe his words. "But you can't be with me if you live in Chicago."

"Why not? What if I moved?"

Her heart somersaulted as she thought of the possibility of Shawn moving. They could date and maybe have a relationship that didn't have so much to do with work. But if she was being honest with herself, that wasn't likely to happen. "Shawn, I don't want you to regret anything. Goodbye will be much easier with no strings attached."

"Listen to me, Carolina." Shawn leaned close and looked directly in her eyes. "You're not getting rid of me." He smiled and pulled her toward him.

She leaned her head into Shawn's chest and let him wrap her in his arms again. His words were her personal fairy tale. Why was her heart torturing her with this possibility that would ultimately end in the same truth that she'd learned long ago? That truth rang in her ears every time she became comfortable: *You can't depend on other people.*

But the power behind that truth was fading and being replaced with the words Shawn had spoken. Why couldn't they be true for her today? If they were true, she would allow herself to fall completely into Shawn's arms. Daniel had already given him his heart. Why couldn't she do the same? The truth was that she loved him, but she was too afraid to say it. "Shawn, I—I care for you too."

Shawn kissed the top of her head. "It's gonna be alright, babe. We're gonna be okay."

Carolina closed her eyes, repeating that phrase over and over in her mind. He'd said, "We're gonna be okay." He'd included himself in her life.

15

Burke's Higher Steps was still in communication with the city's planning and zoning committee through Shawn, and he had his work cut out for him. It seemed like every time they took a step forward, the city found a way to push them two steps back. He pushed his hand through his hair and blew out a breath. He had to make this work for the center, for Carolina and Daniel. It wasn't just the playground that was at stake anymore.

He'd been working on the project for nearly two months now, and decided not to tell Carolina about the problems he'd run into at the planning and zoning office. He'd thought about it a few times, especially when she'd asked him when he thought they'd hear back on the proposal, but he decided to wait until he had more concrete information. No sense in worrying her when she already had enough worries just trying to keep afloat caring for Daniel and paying her monthly rent.

Shawn kept picturing her face when he could give her the news that Burke's Higher Steps had purchased The Heart of Atlanta and the surrounding property, ensuring that refugees could continue to have a safe haven in the city. Shawn grinned and stood taller when he thought of holding Carolina in his arms and sharing smiles with her.

She had been hesitant and disbelieving of his intentions. Either she was a really great actor, or she truly wasn't after Shawn for his money. Every time he thought of his doubts, his stomach twisted. He didn't have any doubts when he concentrated on the feelings he had while kissing Carolina. With a frown, he refocused on work. Things with Carolina were going great. Overanalyzing wouldn't get him any answers.

After he completed another round of phone calls in the city, he checked in with the legal department at Burke's Higher Steps and made a few more phone calls to Lexi in Kauai. Everything appeared to be moving steadily toward the desired result. Lexi was thrilled with the idea that they could control the outcome of the refugee center, especially since they were going to be putting over a million dollars into the program. Shawn still hadn't been given the go-ahead to reveal the total amount, and he felt like a kid on Christmas Eve holding that secret inside. Every time he saw Carolina and how hard she worked alongside Lisette, he was tempted to share the good news, but Lexi's threat kept him from revealing the promised happy ending.

"If you tell them, I'll find a big project for you to work on in Chicago—one that'll take months to complete." Lexi cleared her throat. "But if you really like it in Atlanta, I have a lot more work to do in that area of the country. I need a team leader who can make this arm of our business thrive."

Shawn had thought about the suggested offer many times. Lexi was basically giving him a chance to uproot his life and start over in a new department and a new lifestyle. He cringed when he thought of returning to his corporate life in the Burke Enterprises building in Chicago. The city was wonderful, but he'd never ventured out of his office enough to take part in life. If he had to return, he would do so as a different man. When he'd left the city to head south, he never imagined that he might dread returning alone. Blowing out a breath, Shawn lifted his head toward the gray-blue sky. Could Atlanta become his new home?

On Saturday, Shawn arrived at Carolina's door carrying a bouquet of colorful daisies. The doubts that had been needling him were closed tightly in an imaginary box. Carolina was a beautiful, kind woman, and he'd been given a chance to date her. He didn't want to waste it.

His heart started knocking on the door before he did. He just couldn't seem to get enough of Carolina. He knocked, and Carolina opened the door a few seconds later.

"Hey, babe, I thought of you when I saw these."

Carolina took the flowers and held them to her chest, inhaling deeply. "Thank you. I love all the colors."

She rose up on her tiptoes and kissed Shawn. He wanted to hold her and kiss her longer, but the flowers might get smashed. Carolina stepped back and looked at the flowers, and then back at Shawn. Had she been thinking the same thing? She turned to put the flowers in a vase, with Shawn following close behind her.

"Hey, buddy, I've got something for you too." Shawn held a plastic bag toward Daniel. Daniel skidded forward and pawed through the paper bag with a squeal. He pulled out a small, green John Deere tractor. He looked at the tractor, to Shawn, and then to Carolina as if asking for permission. Shawn glanced at Carolina with a huge grin. "Go ahead and drive it, buddy. It's all yours."

"Daniel, can you tell Shawn thank you?"

Daniel hesitated, and then ran to Shawn and hugged him. "I love you, Shawn."

Warmth pulsed from Shawn's heart, and his throat got a little tight. He hugged Daniel back. "I'm glad you like it."

Carolina chuckled. "I guess that's as good as a thank-you."

"You're lucky, you know," Shawn said. "You get to be with him every day."

"Well, so do you—at least lately."

Shawn nodded. Was he coming on too strong? Maybe Carolina was having doubts about him, although with Daniel's show of affection, Shawn's biggest inadequacy was fading fast. He'd stepped toward Carolina and the idea of a relationship knowing full well that he had no experience parenting, but he'd formed a natural bond with Daniel that pulled at his heartstrings every time he thought about what the future might hold. "I hope you're not getting sick of me yet."

"Never."

There was something about the way she said that word. It hinted that maybe his hopes about her weren't too far-fetched. Everything had happened quickly, much faster than was reasonable, but he loved Carolina. He hadn't figured out all the details yet, but he was considering making some major changes in his career that would enable him to stay in Atlanta with the woman he loved and the son he adored. Even thinking about it scared him a little, and the imaginary box full of doubts rattled, but Shawn smiled and looked straight into Carolina's eyes. Those dark eyes were clear of anything malicious—they were bright with something that Shawn hoped might be love for him.

"I have something special planned for today."

"Just being with you is enough, Shawn. I hope you know that," Carolina said.

Shawn took her hand and tugged her toward him. He kissed her gently, and Carolina softened, deepening the kiss. Shawn broke the kiss and nuzzled her neck. "You make it awful hard for a man to keep his promises," he murmured.

Carolina tipped her head back, her brow furrowing.

"The promises I made to my father, the same ones I made to my God about how I would treat a woman." He kissed her cheek. "I mean to keep those promises."

Carolina stepped back and took hold of both of his hands. She squeezed them, nodding her understanding of what he meant.

"Let's go. Those cloudy skies are threatening rain." Shawn held out his hand toward Daniel. "I want to try to beat the worst of the storm."

They drove out of the city toward Marietta, and he noticed how both Daniel and Carolina looked out the window at the rolling hills and trees that packed the roadway. Daniel drove his toy tractor along his car seat and over the bag of books and crayons Carolina had packed for him.

"Are we there yet?" Daniel asked after they'd driven for a while.

"Almost. Just a few more minutes," Shawn answered. "I'm taking you to Kennesaw Mountain National Battlefield Park." During his search of interesting places in and around Atlanta, he'd discovered the historic park. "This park was the site of a major battle in the Civil War called the Atlanta Campaign." He slowed so that they could read the plaque as they entered the park. He had purchased a picnic lunch at a local sandwich shop, and some treats for dessert. He'd stuffed in a couple blankets and umbrellas just in case. As they got out of the car he looked at the skies and prayed that the rain would wait for him to make this memory for Carolina and Daniel.

"Are you two up for a hike?" Shawn asked as he helped them from the car.

"Yes! Yes!" Daniel jumped up and down.

Carolina laughed, and the trio entered the visitor center to pick up a brochure that outlined the park and hiking trails.

"Let's go!" Daniel cried as soon as they exited the visitor center. He took off running across the stretch of grass in front of them.

Shawn ran after Daniel and scooped him up in his arms. They both laughed as Shawn twirled Daniel around. Carolina caught up and took hold of Daniel's hand.

"You can run, but you have to make sure we can still see you. Okay?"

Daniel frowned. "Okay, but don't go so slow."

Shawn raised his eyebrows and took Carolina's hand. "I'll hurry her along."

Carolina rolled her eyes, but Shawn could tell she was

enjoying the day. They hiked up Pigeon Trail about halfway before Shawn suggested they stop. "Let's head back down the trail for our picnic." He worried that the heavy gray clouds wouldn't hold for much longer.

"This is a beautiful park," Carolina said. "There are a lot of really old buildings around Atlanta. I've heard about them, but haven't been to see many of the monuments." She looked down and licked her lips. "I never had much schooling here in America."

Shawn nodded. "I wondered if you had, because you're so well-spoken."

"Thank you," Carolina said, ducking her head.

"This place made me think about how American history is such an important part of my life here, and how different it would be if I'd come from somewhere else—like the refugees."

"Like me," Carolina spoke softly. She looked up at him in a way that made his heart pound. He wanted to do this right—to share a part of him with Carolina and Daniel.

"Yes." Shawn squeezed her hand. "You've told me some things about your country, now I want to share a little about mine." Shawn pointed out some information about the park in the brochure. He also pulled up facts about the Civil War on his phone and read them to Carolina. He explained how important the Civil War was as a turning point in the United States, a time when everyone had to decide if all men were created equal. He hoped that Carolina would see the significance of it. As he explained the differences between the North and the South, he saw understanding in her eyes.

"So the Civil War was important, because my skin isn't white, and neither is my son's, but this war allows us to do all the same things." Carolina held out her arm, the coffee-colored skin a shade lighter than Daniel's.

Shawn nodded. He held out his arm, the pale skin contrasting from Carolina's. He didn't see it as different —he saw it as a beautiful combination that he wanted to explore. "The war was only the beginning. A lot of battles still had to be fought through the years. It will never be perfect for all people, but it's something we can always strive for. Something we can remember. People fought for that freedom, died for it, and live for it. It still matters."

"Thanks, Shawn." Carolina put her hand to her face and smiled.

"Enough of the history lessons." He leaned over and kissed Carolina. Her mouth softened against his, and he pulled her into his arms, deepening the kiss.

"Why do you do that?" Daniel asked innocently.

Shawn leaned back, but kept his arm around Carolina. "Do what?"

"Eat my mom?"

Carolina laughed so hard she snorted, and that made Shawn laugh. It was a good thing they were laughing, because he had no idea how to answer that question.

Daniel laughed and rolled around in the grass, giggling. Shawn tickled Daniel and then Carolina, and she squealed and rolled out of his grasp. He followed her, pinning her down on the grass and kissing her until the giggles subsided. Daniel was busy doing somersaults by then and didn't seem to mind that Shawn was "eating" his mom again.

Carolina wrapped her arms around his neck, kissing him, and then put her hand on his cheek. "If this is a picnic, we should probably eat sandwiches, right?" She waggled her eyebrows, and Shawn chuckled.

He rolled over with a groan and looked up at the clouds that were growing darker by the minute. "I think we'd better eat fast."

Just as they were finishing the last bites of their sandwich, the sky broke open and started pouring rain. Carolina hurriedly stuffed everything into the bag, and they ran for the car, shrieking and laughing. Shawn turned the heater up in the car to help dry out their clothes. Once they had stopped dripping, he passed out the cupcakes that he'd purchased for the picnic.

"Thanks, Shawn. I love cupcakes!" Daniel said as he took a huge bite of the cupcake with blue frosting and sprinkles.

"Yes, thanks. This was a lot of fun. I'm glad to see part of Georgia that I hadn't before."

"Well, how would you two feel about going to a movie?"

In the breath of hesitation it took for Carolina to agree, Shawn guessed that it had probably been many years since she'd gone to a movie.

She looked down and pressed her teeth against her bottom lip. "I've never taken Daniel to the theater. But he loves cartoons."

"Well, that's perfect, because there's a new Disney cartoon playing. I'd love to see his face when those characters come on the big screen."

Carolina smiled, and Shawn put the car into drive and headed toward the movie theater. The magic of possibilities ignited new excitement in his soul. He wanted to show Carolina and Daniel the world, but most of all, he wanted to show them his love.

16

The following week, Carolina finished up with her morning duties early at the center. Shawn was busy working on some things outside of the office, and Carolina wanted to help out with the new plans for the center. She found Lisette in her office, checking items off a clipboard.

"We still haven't heard back on the proposal for the playground. Do you mind if I go down to the city office and check that out?" Carolina asked.

"Sure, that's a great idea," Lisette replied. "I was going to follow up on that myself, but I couldn't nail Shawn down."

"He's been pretty busy," Carolina said.

"I know. That's because someone around here eats up all of his spare time." Lisette winked and pulled a sheaf of papers out of the filing cabinet.

"I'll take Daniel with me. We'll probably be gone a couple hours," Carolina said, avoiding the conversation about the relationship Lisette had hinted at, even though her stomach somersaulted at the mention of his name. Shawn had opened up her heart to a world where love was possible, and Carolina couldn't stand being apart from him.

"Are you sure you don't want to wait for Shawn?" Lisette tapped a pen against the pile of papers. "I could use some help sorting through these documents."

"As fun as that sounds, I think I'll pass. See if you can get Ammon to help you. He likes that sort of stuff." Carolina waved as she grabbed her bag and headed to the play area for Daniel.

A few minutes later, they walked down to the bus station, the sun peeking through a gray sky.

"Why can't we ride with Shawn?" Daniel asked.

"Because Shawn is busy working."

"I like Shawn," Daniel said as he skipped along.

"Me too." Carolina took his hand and quickened her step to keep up with him. Her heart fluttered when she thought about Shawn and the way he had connected with her son. It more than fluttered when she thought about the way he had kissed her the night before, and how she couldn't wait to see him again tonight.

Her smile widened as she thought about the time they had spent together. Hopefully she would find some good news today to share with Shawn about the plans for the playground at the center. Carolina had never been inside the planning and zoning office of the city. She walked across the marble foyer and into a beautiful office with a large window overlooking a copse of trees. "I'm here to check on a proposal for a new playground," Carolina said.

The secretary was an older woman with gray hair tinted at the edges in a bluish hue. She pushed her glasses up the bridge of her nose. "Let me check if Mr. Lawson is free."

A moment later, the secretary directed Carolina and Daniel down a short hallway toward an office with a sign that read, *Planning and Zoning Director*. The secretary opened the door and showed Carolina in.

A short man with dark skin and a bristly mustache stood and held out his hand. "Max Lawson. How can I help you?"

Carolina shook his hand and sat down. "I work at the Heart of Atlanta Refugee Center. We turned in a proposal for a new playground a couple months ago. I wanted to see if you could update me on where the proposal is or when a decision might be made."

Max furrowed his brow and clicked a few things on his computer. Then he nodded and mumbled something to himself before looking up at Carolina. "Yes, your playground proposal is on hold because the building and surrounding areas have been sold. I thought you'd been notified. I'm sorry that the news slipped through the cracks somehow."

Carolina's jaw dropped. She blinked several times, wondering if she'd heard the man right. "Sold? The refugee center—the building—has been sold?"

"Yes. Your director will have to meet with the new owners to discuss everything. There were several new developers looking at the area, so they may have ideas of where to relocate the center in the future."

The room seemed to tilt, and Carolina gripped the arms of the chair. A buzzing sound filled her ears. "No, that can't be right."

"I'm afraid it is. These things happen all the time, especially in a city as old as Atlanta. Change is the one constant." Max re-stacked the pile of papers and cleared his throat. "If you talk to your director, she should be able to give you more information."

"No. That's fine." It wasn't fine. Nothing was fine. What was going to happen to the center, to all of the people who depended on it? Carolina rode the bus back to the center in a daze. She kept swallowing back the tears and put on a happy face for Daniel. Maybe Mr. Lawson was wrong. Maybe when she spoke with Lisette, they would discover he'd been misinformed. Carolina distracted herself by playing cars with Daniel as they traveled back toward the center.

When she returned, she set Daniel up with a cartoon in the play area and returned to her desk. She entered the office and saw Shawn standing next to her desk. His face lit up with a smile when he saw her, but he frowned as he seemed to take in her appearance. "What's wrong?"

Carolina couldn't swallow the tears any longer. The ball of prickly emotion she'd been swallowing for the past half hour broke free, and she sank into a chair. "We hadn't heard back about the playground proposal, so I went to check. The director told me that the building and surrounding property have been sold." Carolina choked on a sob, and Shawn handed her a Kleenex.

"Sold? Are you sure?" He pushed his hand through his hair. "That can't be right."

Carolina sniffled. "That's what I said, but Mr. Lawson told me to talk to Lisette. He said she would have all the information."

"Lisette left for the day. She had a meeting to attend." Shawn handed Carolina another tissue. "This can't be right. He said they were only considering the area."

Carolina lifted her head. "What do you mean? Did you know about this?"

Shawn clenched his jaw. "When I turned in the proposal, Mr. Lawson said they were looking at building new schools in the area." He wiped a hand over his beard and hesitated, squinting his eyes. "He said the center was one of their top choices. He made it sound like it was a long way off. How could it have sold so quickly?"

"Shawn, you knew about this?" Carolina cried. "Months ago? And you didn't tell me?"

"No, I didn't want to worry you." He pushed his hand through his hair again and stood up, pacing back and forth. "I knew it wouldn't happen. I talked to Lexi. I don't know what happened."

Carolina stood up as well, holding onto the back of the chair. "Why didn't you tell me? Shawn, if they close the center, I won't have a job anymore. I'll have to move."

Shawn stopped pacing and came to her side, placing his hands on her arms. "No, even if they close the center, it wouldn't be for some time. The center would relocate."

"You don't know that!" Carolina cried. "If I lose my job, I don't have a safety net." Carolina held the tissue to her mouth to cover another sob.

"We'll get this figured out. You're not going to lose your job."

"How could you keep this from me? This center is my life."

Shawn opened and closed his mouth. "Because. I couldn't tell you. It wasn't my secret to share."

Carolina pushed out her hand. "Stop. I don't want to hear anymore." She picked up her bag and walked out of the office.

"Carolina, where are you going? Don't leave." Shawn walked quickly to her side. "Let's figure this out."

But Carolina didn't stop. Her head throbbed with the anguish and betrayal she felt. Shawn knew the center was in danger, and he'd done nothing! She grabbed Daniel and hefted the heavy child under her arms and walked quickly out of the center with Shawn following after her, pleading, "Let me explain. Let me make a few phone calls. We can make this right."

Carolina spun around. "If you knew it was up for sale, why didn't you buy the property? It would've been nothing for you to buy it."

"Carolina!" Shawn called after her as she hurried to catch a bus. The motor revved as it prepared to pull away. Carolina waved, and the driver let her and Daniel on. Before Shawn could say anymore, they were traveling away from the refugee center. A tiny voice told her that she'd acted unfairly. What had Shawn ever done that even hinted at being dishonest?

On the ride home, Carolina buried her face in her hands and sobbed. An elderly woman next to her patted her back. "It's all right dear. It's never as bad as it seems." The woman handed Daniel a few chocolate-covered raisins, and he ate quietly. Carolina suffocated on the crushed dreams she had pinned on Shawn. Somehow he knew what was happening—he knew more than he was telling. And he had chosen not to share with her.

❧ 17 ❧

Shawn raced after Carolina, but she was on the bus before he could say another word. Buy the place? How much money did she think he had? Shawn shook his head and walked dejectedly back toward the center. The sun came out from behind a cloud, and he squinted at the bright light. And then the truth hit him. Carolina must think that he was as wealthy as the Burkes. Shawn closed his eyes and tipped his head back. It made sense now. He worked closely with both Lexi and Jordan, who were billionaires. Carolina must have thought he was part-owner of the company or something. That explained her reaction.

He pulled his cell phone out and called Lexi, but there was no answer. He glanced at his watch and cursed. It was early morning in Kauai. Lexi never took calls during her morning routine.

With a groan, Shawn dialed the legal department of Burke Enterprises and asked to speak to Alex. One minute, he'd been smiling at Carolina, excited to tell her about plans for funding the center's new skills department, the next his world had imploded. Something must have gone very wrong with the purchase of the land. The last Shawn had heard, the contract was in review, and everything had been given the green light. Carolina didn't give him a chance to explain, but he was going to take the time now to figure out the details.

"Shawn, how can I help you?" Alex asked when he answered the phone.

"I'm praying you can help me." Shawn looked down the street to where the bus had disappeared, carrying Carolina and Daniel. "I think I need a miracle."

❦

By the time they arrived at the apartment, Carolina's well of tears had run dry. She made Daniel a snack, and then washed her face, holding a washcloth over her puffy eyes.

"Why are you sad, Mommy? Why did you yell at Shawn?"

Carolina's lip trembled. "Mommy had a really hard day at work today."

"You should tell Shawn sorry." Daniel tilted his head to one side, watching Carolina for a reaction.

She nodded. "I shouldn't have yelled at him." She

couldn't bring herself to agree with Daniel. She wouldn't apologize to Shawn for what he did. As soon as she thought that, her stomach twisted with a warning. She hadn't given Shawn a chance to explain, and he had been genuinely worried. Carolina pressed her lips together. She was afraid, but she shouldn't have acted rashly.

Her instinct to protect herself and Daniel was the reason she'd survived on her own. Her grandmother had told her never to let fear make choices, but she hadn't followed that advice earlier. Fear had obliterated the trust she'd built with Shawn. Carolina slumped onto the couch, leaning her head back to look at the stained ceiling. She had sat here on this couch, cuddling with Shawn while he reassured her that she would never have to worry about being safe. He promised her that he would take care of her and Daniel. Had Carolina pushed away the safety net that God had given her when she met Shawn?

Later that day, Shawn finally got through to Lexi. He'd found the information he needed, with help from the legal department, and he had a tiny hope that Carolina might be able to forgive him when he told her what he'd discovered.

"I have to make this right," Shawn told Lexi, gripping the phone to his ear.

"You've got this," Lexi replied. "If this girl is as special as you've said, she'll let you explain. And then she'll love you for it."

Shawn blew out a breath. "I hope so. I think this whole time Carolina thought I was a billionaire."

Lexi chuckled. "That's a good one, Shawn."

"No, really. She asked me why I didn't just buy the refugee center. I think because I talked about you and

Jordan so much, she must have just assumed I was higher up in the company."

"And now you're worried that this whole time she's only been after your money." Lexi spoke gently, but her words still ran a jagged edge against Shawn's heart.

"No, she's not like that," Shawn said. "At least, I don't think she is."

"The only way to find out is to ask her," Lexi replied. "You have to come clean with everything, so you might as well cover your finances too. You're not a billionaire, but you aren't a pauper, either."

Shawn rolled his eyes. "Lexi, you always give it to me straight."

"I just hope she'll give you another chance."

"Me too."

❦ 19 ❦

Carolina got up the next morning and wondered if she should just stay home. She didn't want to face Shawn or feel the raw edges of her heart, but she prepared to go to work at the center anyway. She had prayed constantly for a miracle, asking God to show her the way so that she could continue to provide for her son. She'd woken during the night, and a feeling of peace came over her. Now, in the early morning light, she felt that somehow, everything would work out. It had to, because she didn't want to live with this hurt. She poured Daniel a bowl of Rice Chex and sat next to him slicing bananas on top of the cereal.

Yesterday she'd surveyed their apartment and tried to prepare herself mentally for moving once again. They didn't have very many things to pack, so that part of moving wasn't difficult. She'd been on a waiting list to get into this apartment because she liked the schools in the area and was trying to plan ahead for Daniel. There was a great bilingual school that taught both Spanish and English, and she wanted Daniel to have that opportunity. All of her planning and dreams would be for nothing if they had to start over in a new neighborhood.

"Go and brush your teeth, Daniel." Carolina forced herself to move forward, focusing on the mundane. "Do you want Mommy to help you today?"

Daniel shook his head, still munching his cereal. "I can do it. Is Shawn coming today?"

Carolina closed her eyes and shook her head. "I don't know if we'll see very much of Shawn anymore."

"Why? I love Shawn."

Before she could answer, there was a knock at the door. Carolina's heart jumped into her throat as she approached the peephole. Peering through, she felt another jolt of surprise when she saw Shawn standing nervously outside her front door. Should she let him in? He didn't appear angry. A flicker of hope flared in Carolina's chest—a hope that she could apologize and make things right. But what if he had come to say goodbye?

He must've heard her approach, because he spoke quietly, "Please let me in. I have some wonderful news I want to share with you."

She opened the door. "Hi. I'm so sorry about yesterday. I was afraid, but I know it wasn't your fault." Her words tumbled over each other.

Shawn stepped inside, offering her a smile that didn't reach his eyes. She didn't blame him for acting reticent. He swallowed and rolled his shoulders back. "I just wanted to tell you that the Heart of Atlanta Center is safe."

Carolina struggled to find words as the flicker of hope fanned into flame. "How do you know?"

Shawn smiled, and this time it did reach his eyes. "Because my foundation—the foundation I work for—bought all of the property. They wanted to make sure that the Center continues running."

Carolina put a hand on her forehead and breathed in slowly. "Then why did the director at the city office tell me it was sold?"

Shawn grinned. "Because it *was* sold. To Burke's Higher Steps. The only information I had before was that the city was looking at a few options to build new schools and had considered the center as one of those options."

Carolina tilted her head. "I don't understand why you couldn't have told me that."

"I guess I should have, but at the time, I didn't want to worry you. I'd only known you a few days back then." Shawn reached for her hand, gently clasping her fingers. "As soon as I found out about the city's plans, I called

Lexi and asked her if she could buy the property through her foundation. Things were put in place quickly, but quick in real estate still means several weeks. Just last week, I was sure that I'd have good news for you soon. So when you went to the office and told me that the property had been sold, I guessed the worst. I was afraid something had gone wrong and we missed our chance."

He smiled and squeezed her hand. "Yesterday, I was on the phone verifying everything for most of the day. I wanted to come over here in the middle of the night and tell you the good news, but I decided it was better to wait."

Carolina gave him a shaky smile that hid the shame blooming in her chest. "I can't believe it. So the center really is safe? It will keep running?"

"That's right. But there's something else I wanted to clear up."

Carolina shook her head, interrupting him. "I'm sorry I got mad at you, Shawn. I was afraid. Fear does crazy things to me. I feel horrible."

Shawn shook his head. "No, it's okay. I understand." He leaned in closer to her, his eyes softening. "The thing is, what you said yesterday about me buying the property. Did you think I was a billionaire? All this time?" He pressed his lips together as if it pained him to ask the question.

Carolina's eyes widened. First she accused him of

betraying her trust, and now she'd insulted him by assuming his level of wealth. He probably had come to say goodbye. "Well, yeah. Lisette said something about the Burkes' and your company. She said they were billionaires. I just figured you were too."

Shawn laughed. "I'm not a billionaire, Carolina. I'm a regular guy. I'm successful and have worked really hard, so I've earned a good amount of money. I used to think I wanted to be a billionaire, but not anymore."

Carolina wasn't sure what to say. She felt her cheeks heat with embarrassment. What if Shawn thought she was only interested in his money all this time? "It doesn't matter to me."

"Are you sure? I was worried that maybe you thought..." he trailed off.

Carolina's stomach lurched. "You worried that maybe I was only interested in you for your money?" The shame she felt was edged in anger that Shawn could think that, but the reasonable part of her brain took control. She didn't allow herself to give in to those emotions. Yesterday, she had jumped to conclusions and accused Shawn wrongfully. Of course he would have doubts about her motives now.

"I really didn't believe that you would ever do something like that, but I wanted to be sure." Shawn swallowed, his fingers still tracing hers.

"After the way I acted, I deserve your doubts." She

waved her other hand around her apartment. "I'm sure you probably think that because of how we live." She bit her bottom lip, unsure of what she could say to prove to Shawn what she felt in her heart.

"Carolina, I love you. I had doubts because of some of my past dating experiences, but I kept telling myself that I knew your heart. I wanted to be sure. Can you understand?"

Carolina sucked in a breath. He loved her? She smiled, a joy pulsing from her heart. "I love you too."

Shawn pulled her into a hug, squeezing her to his chest. He kissed the side of her head and laughed. "I thought I lost you. It scared me. Made me realize how much I want to be with you and Daniel."

Carolina felt Daniel hugging the sides of their legs. "I love you too. Are you going to be my daddy?" Daniel asked.

Carolina laughed at the surprised look on Shawn's face that quickly turned to tenderness. He glanced at Carolina and she nodded. "I'd like that very much," Shawn said. He knelt down and hugged Daniel.

Carolina's eyes filled with tears. Shawn stood and touched the side of her face, wiping away a tear. "Don't cry. You don't have to be afraid anymore. Let me take care of you and love you."

Carolina leaned up and kissed him softly. "These are happy tears."

"Te amo, mi princesa. Serás mio?" Shawn spoke in Spanish.

Carolina chuckled. "That's impressive."

"Well, I mean it," Shawn said, holding her close. "I love you, my princess. Will you be mine?" He repeated the sentence in English.

Carolina smiled. "Sí, te amo. Forever."

❧ 20 ❧

Shawn worked with Carolina at the Heart of Atlanta Refugee Center for another week, putting the last details into place for the funding to come through for Burke's Higher Steps. Everyone at the center was in a celebratory mood, and each day Carolina's smile seemed to grow wider. Shawn loved watching the weight lifting from her shoulders as she came to trust him and her bright future.

Every night after he dropped Carolina off, Shawn returned to his hotel room and researched the plans he had made that would change the trajectory of his life. If someone had asked him last year if he'd ever think of leaving Burke Enterprises and his high-rise office in Chicago, Shawn would've laughed at them. But now, after spending a few months in Atlanta, Carolina had helped him change his perspective. It was a hard decision, but he put in his notice at Burke Enterprises. Lexi offered him a position for the foundation she'd created under an arm of Burke Enterprises. She wanted him to work from Atlanta at Burke's Higher Steps.

One of the first projects he planned to set up would feature Carolina as a success story. He wanted the world to know how a young woman arriving as a refugee and orphan could make good choices and influence others. Carolina was apprehensive about it, but Shawn had noted a flicker of excitement in her eyes when he told her about the idea.

Shawn found a realtor who worked quickly to scour the area around Atlanta for the perfect house in the perfect neighborhood, yet still within thirty minutes of the refugee center. Carolina trusted him, but that trust was fragile. At times, he almost could see the doubts flicker across her face as if she couldn't believe that life could be that good to her. He wanted to prove to her, once and for all, that he would be there for her. So Shawn purchased a three-bedroom house at the end of a cul-de-sac. The home had a fenced-in yard and a great view of a wooded area behind the property. Located about twenty minutes away from the center, it was in a great school district. Once everything was in place, Shawn was ready to step out on the precipice and take the leap to show his love to Carolina. If she still needed time, then he would have a place to live while he made the transition to his new job in Atlanta, but he prayed that she felt the same love and desire for him that he did for her.

It was a Saturday morning when he pulled up in front of Carolina's apartment. He took a moment to notice the rundown building with chipped and peeling paint. The concrete had crumbling edges, and there was litter in the corners near the entrance. He heard sirens in the distance and noticed the trash in the streets. He climbed the steps, noting the smell of smoke and old food as he approached Carolina's apartment. He hoped that his plan would work. He knocked on the door, and Carolina answered with her usual smile.

"Hey, babe. I love seeing your face," Shawn said. He walked inside and kissed Carolina, lingering over her lips a moment longer than he usually allowed himself to.

Carolina pulled back, her cheeks darkening with a blush. "Good morning to you too."

Shawn grinned and put his arm around her. "How are you doing?"

Carolina giggled. "I'm fine. Are you going to tell me why you look so happy?"

"Can't a guy be happy just seeing his girl?"

Daniel ran through the room holding up a toy airplane buzzing around cheerfully. "Hi Shawn! I'm flying. Watch out!" He buzzed by Shawn and Carolina, and Shawn felt the familiar surge of love towards the boy who he hoped would soon be his son.

"Have I told you how much I love you?"

Carolina smiled. "A few times. But I wouldn't mind hearing it again."

"I love you." Shawn's heart beat with the truth of the words he spoke to Carolina. "I want to always see that happy smile on your face. I want to take care of you and Daniel. Will you let me?"

She nodded. "You have taken care of us. You saved the center. I have a job that I love, and Daniel and I don't have to move."

"Well, about that," Shawn lowered his voice. "I have a proposal for you."

Carolina's eyes widened, and Shawn chuckled. He pulled out the set of keys from his pocket and held them in front of her face. "I bought a house on the outskirts of Atlanta. It's in a great neighborhood, and it has three bedrooms. I want to know if you'll help me take care of it."

Carolina looked at the keys, and then at Shawn, puzzled. "What are you asking me?"

"I don't want to rush things. I don't want to scare you, but I also don't want to let you go." Shawn put his hands on her upper arms and looked into her eyes. "I bought a house, and I want you to live in it. I have to go back to Chicago for a few weeks to finish out some projects at work. But I've given them my notice. Three weeks to a month at most is all I will be gone. And then I'm moving to Atlanta permanently."

Carolina put a hand over her mouth, but it didn't

cover the edges of her upturned lips. She gave a little squeal of joy. "This is real?"

Shawn nodded. "Before I leave, I want to help you and Daniel move into the house. I want you to set things up the way that you've always dreamed. To live the life you've always dreamed of."

"And then you come back and ...?" She worried her bottom lip over her teeth.

Shawn pulled in a breath as he fished in his pocket and pulled out a small, white box. He sank to his knee and looked up at Carolina. "When I get back, I'll stay at a hotel and hopefully it won't be long, but it depends on your answer to this question." He lifted the lid of the box to reveal a diamond ring. "Carolina Diaz, will you marry me? Will you be my wife and let me be the father to your son?"

Carolina smiled, her white teeth bright against her dark skin. "Yes!" she half sobbed, half cried. "Yes, I want to be with you."

Shawn stood and pulled her into a hug. He kissed her, moving his mouth against hers as he whispered his love to her again. Then he helped slide the diamond solitaire onto Carolina's small finger. She looked down at the ring and back at Shawn. "Is this real? I want to believe it, but I'm afraid I'll wake up, and it will all be a dream."

Shawn took her hand, squeezing her fingertips. "It's real. My love is real. Our life is going to be wonderful."

Carolina looked at the ring again, and then lifted her

hand to touch his cheek, her fingers moving against his beard. She leaned forward and kissed him. "Tienes mi corazón. You have my heart."

"I'll keep it safe forever," he murmured as he pulled her close for another kiss.

EPILOGUE- THREE MONTHS LATER

Carolina kissed her husband in the back of the limo as the driver pulled away from the reception hall. Shawn nuzzled her neck and she giggled, feeling like the happiness bubbling up inside her could carry them away to the island in the Bahamas where Shawn planned to take her for their honeymoon.

"I can't believe I'm married. I feel like a princess." Carolina fingered her satin gown and admired the wedding band Shawn had added to her engagement ring that morning.

"You are my queen," Shawn murmured as he kissed her earlobe.

Carolina turned and caught his mouth, kissing him until he moaned softly. "Can't he drive any faster?"

She giggled, a thousand butterflies of anticipation and

joy fluttering through her middle. "I'm so glad that Daniel took to your mother so quickly."

"Me, too. My mom seemed really happy about her new grandson," Shawn said.

Shawn's parents had been wary at first about the whirlwind romance of their son and his fiancé from Cuba, but Daniel had captured their hearts immediately. Carolina looked forward to getting to know her in-laws better and being a part of a whole family again.

Shawn's parents were taking Daniel to a beach house for a week on the coast of Georgia. They were overjoyed to be babysitting him while Shawn and Carolina went on their ten day honeymoon. Carolina looked forward to having parents again, and especially grandparents for Daniel and future children. Her stomach flipped again as she thought of building a family with Shawn.

The limo driver pulled up to their house and opened the door for Carolina. Shawn took her hand as they walked up the front steps to their home. When they reached the front porch, he swooped her up into his arms. Carolina cried out in surprise. "What are you doing?"

"I'm carrying you over the threshold and into my life forever." He pushed open the door with his foot, holding her close against his chest.

Carolina wrapped her arms around his neck and rested her head on his shoulder as he stepped inside the house. He cradled her in his arms, turning slowly to push the door closed. Carolina looked into his face and saw the desire there. Her heart beat with the same desire to be with her husband. She felt safe, loved, and protected in Shawn's arms and she didn't want him to let go.

"We're going to have a beautiful life together, aren't we?" she whispered.

Shawn lowered her feet to the ground, but pulled her close to him once again. "Yes, and every day I'll thank God that a little refugee from Cuba rescued my heart."

Carolina smiled as Shawn lowered his head to kiss her, pulling her toward the bedroom and their happily ever after.

If you enjoyed this story, read the Burke Billionaire Romance Series to learn more about Jordan and Lexi Burke. Visit www. rachellechristensen.com and keep turning the page for a sneak peek!

SNEAK PEEK OF HAWAIIAN MASQUERADE

Lexi stared at the tube of cadmium red oil paint hanging from the shelf, remembering how expensive that color had seemed in college. She grabbed it and ten additional tubes in a rainbow of colors—the first step on a new path in life. The squeaking wheel of the shopping cart gave voice to the trepidation crawling up her spine, telling her she was nuts for leaving behind a life that most people claimed they wanted. But Lexi knew something that most people didn't: millions and millions of dollars did not create a wellspring of happiness. Cold hard cash was, in fact, cold and hard.

Kauai was not cold. The brilliant sunshine and perfumed air was freely available to everyone on the island. Roadways were drenched in color from vibrant greens to bright pinks and accented with the red dirt Kauai was known for. Lexi studied the brushes available and chose a long-handled round brush that would help her recreate the beautiful landscapes of the island. Now if she could find a few canvases, she would be ready to paint on the beach outside her home. She turned down another aisle and saw a display of white rectangles and squares. They were wrapped in plastic, but Lexi ran her finger along the edges; the rough feel of a blank canvas and the possibility it represented brought back pleasant memories.

A toddler's shrill cry snapped her out of her musings. She steered her cart around a stack of twelve-by-eighteen-inch canvases and found the source. The little girl couldn't have been more than two years old, tiny with fine black hair pulled back in pigtails. Her red hibiscus-print dress set off dark caramel skin, and even as her wail intensified, Lexi found herself admiring the pretty Polynesian girl.

That's when she noticed that the toddler was alone. Lexi glanced around, but this area of the store was empty. She stepped forward carefully and crouched in front of the girl. "Sweetie, are you lost?"

As soon as the words left her mouth, the little girl held out her arms and reached for Lexi. She sniffled, melting Lexi's heart as she carefully picked up the child. She looked down the aisle, hoping to see the little girl's mother, but at the same time nervous that the mother would think her daughter was being kidnapped. Lexi patted the girl's back, and she snuggled closer. Swallowing against the sudden lump in her throat, Lexi focused on the task at hand.

Turning slowly to scan the store again, she saw a man with dark hair, a chiseled jawline, and a worried crease in his forehead. He was tall with golden-brown skin and wore a green tank top that showed off his finely sculpted biceps. Something shifted in Lexi's heart. It thumped hard twice, and blood rose to her cheeks. The man stared back at her, his face open, revealing an arc of emotions as he took in the sight of the little girl and Lexi—wonder, admiration, curiosity, and something else she couldn't define.

She stepped forward, eyebrows raised in question. "Is she yours?"

His dark hair was spiked on top and close-shaven on the sides. He sported a bit of scruff that Lexi could only describe as sexy. One side of his mouth lifted, and he shook his head. "No, is she lost?"

"Yes, she was crying right over here, and I've stayed put for a minute hoping her mom would show up looking for her."

He turned around in a slow circle, repeating the search Lexi had undertaken moments before, having a better view over the shelves because he was taller. Oh, so tall and sculpted. "I can help you find her parents. This store isn't that big. Maybe they haven't missed her yet."

Lexi's brow furrowed in protest as she struggled to rein in her emotions. It had been at least three minutes since she'd heard the toddler's cries, and five minutes was like an eternity in a child's world—surely it would feel just as long for a frantic parent searching for her child. She gently patted the girl's back. "It's okay, sweetie, I know what it feels like to be lost," she murmured. Then she realized that the man was standing close enough to hear her. She straightened, cleared her throat, and spoke louder. "We'll help you."

The man pointed to the other side of the store. "I'll go this way, you go that way?"

"That's a good idea." Lexi smiled, and her stomach flipped when the man returned her smile. The little girl moved her head, quiet and warm in Lexi's arms.

The man walked quickly across the store, and Lexi went in the other direction. There was only one other shopper, an old man with a handful of charcoal and sketch pads. Lexi smiled at him, and he winked at her and the little girl. "Beautiful kaikamahine."

Lexi nodded, appreciating the melodic Hawaiian language. The man saw them as mother and daughter, which was a stretch considering Lexi's fair skin, blond hair, and green eyes. She held the child close. They were two lost souls trying to find something to keep them safe. Lexi was certain she'd find the little girl's mother, but what could Lexi find that would fill the need in her heart?

"Here she is," someone said from behind Lexi. She turned around and saw that the dark-haired man was leading a Polynesian woman with long dark hair toward her. "Safe and sound."

"Keilani! Oh, baby," the woman said. "I'm so glad you're okay."

The little girl immediately sat up and reached her arms out. She cried for a few seconds, clinging to her mother, clutching her light cotton shirt.

"Mahalo. Oh, thank you so much for finding my baby," the woman gushed.

"She's a sweetheart," Lexi said. "She wanted me to hold her, and that seemed to help while we looked for you."

"One minute she was there, and then she was gone. You know how kids are." The woman patted her daughter's back. "Keilani, say thank you to the beautiful lady who found you," the woman said, looking down at her daughter with a smile.

The toddler looked at Lexi and held her hand out, moving it back and forth. Then she giggled and blew Lexi a kiss.

Lexi pretended to catch the kiss in the air and patted her cheek. "Thank you, Keilani. Have fun shopping."

She waved at the little girl, then let her hand drop to her side. That's when she noticed the man who had helped her standing quietly next to the end cap of paintbrushes on aisle seven. "You really get the credit for finding her," Lexi said. "Thanks for hunting down the lost mother."

He grinned. "Glad to help out a tourist when I can."

"But I'm not a tourist," Lexi replied. "I just moved here."

One eyebrow lifted, and Lexi noticed a shift in his brown eyes, as if he were seeing her for the first time. He held out his hand. "That's great news. Aloha, and welcome to Kauai. I'm Derek Mitchell."

They shook hands, and a sensation like warm, salty spray went up her arm. When they broke contact, she immediately craved his touch again. What was happening to her? The first hot guy to shake her hand had her thinking of moonlight walks on the beach and kisses in the sand. She decided that she was smitten with the *idea* of this Hawaiian guy. She needed a can of chocolate-covered macadamia nuts and a long bath, not a man. Still, she smiled broadly and returned the introduction. "I'm Lexi Burke, no longer from Chicago."

Derek wrinkled his nose. "Man, that place is cold. Good choice coming here in March. The weather will only get better from now until October."

"I'm counting on it," Lexi replied.

"Are you an artist?" Derek asked, motioning to the growing stack of supplies in Lexi's cart, which she'd left in the middle of the aisle.

"I wish." Lexi laughed as she grabbed the handle. "Maybe in a different lifetime—or maybe now. I love art, and I need to refocus some of my energy. Drawing and painting used to be a passion of mine, before the nine-to-five killed it."

Derek nodded. "I get that. The good thing about this place is it unwinds all that tension, and creativity leaks out from everywhere." He tipped his head to the side. "Since you're new, I'll let you in on a secret. Drive over to Hanapepe tomorrow—Friday night is the local art night—and you'll see what I mean."

"Hmm, I may just do that." Lexi gave Derek her canned response to every invite from the male species. And then she realized that he was being friendly. Maybe she could go . . . but then she might run into him, and he was too good-looking with that bronzed skin and his relaxed stance that seemed to say, *I don't have any idea what my looks do to your pulse rate.* Yep. Derek was on her list of things not to encounter in Kauai. Her fingertips drummed along the plastic-wrapped handle of her shopping cart, trying to keep up with her racing heart. It was time to make a quick exit. "Thanks again for your help. Maybe I'll see you around the island sometime."

"Good luck with the painting." Derek lifted one hand and let it fall. He had a stack of frames tucked under his other arm.

After checking out and packing the supplies into her Jeep, Lexie wished she hadn't been so skittish around Derek and missed the opportunity to reciprocate his interest in her new hobby. He'd spoken about creativity, and judging by the frames and his knowledge of the Hanapepe street fair, he was probably an artist himself. There she was, thinking about him again. Derek was just another piece of man candy Lexi didn't want to taste, even if he'd been kind and genuine at the store. She shouldn't be mean to him just because she carried a chip on her shoulder the size of the Sears Tower. She could give him the benefit of the doubt. Derek was quite possibly delicious on the inside, too.

Then again, so was the authentic Hawaiian shaved ice Lexi was going to pick up at Hee Fat General Store. Yes, ice covered in sugar sitting on top of a mountain of thick ice cream would definitely do the trick to keep Lexi's mind from wandering into dangerous territory.

Keep reading *Hawaiian Masquerade* right HERE

Enjoy the first three books in the Burke Billionaire Romance Series with more to come!
Hawaiian Masquerade
The Billionaire's Stray Heart
The Refugee's Billionaire

Photo by Erin Summerill

Rachelle writes mystery/suspense, clean romance, and women's fiction. She is the mother of a large family and she solves the case of the missing shoe on a daily basis. She enjoys raising chickens, laughing with her family, and traveling with her husband. She graduated cum laude from Utah State University with a degree in psychology and a minor in music.

Rachelle is the award-winning author of over twenty books, including *The Soldier's Bride (a Kindle Scout Selection)*, the Rone award winner for mystery, *River Whispers, Diamond Rings Are Deadly Things, Hawaiian Masquerade,* and *the Echo Ridge Romance series*. Her novella, "Silver Cascade Secrets," was included in the Rone Award–winning *Timeless Romance Anthology, Fall Collection*.

Join Rachelle's VIP mailing list to learn more about upcoming books and get your free book at www.rachellechristensen.com.

Free Book!

Thrills for the Heart

FOR A LIMITED TIME

Sign up for Rachelle's
VIP Mailing List
to get your *FREE* book.

★ ★ ★ ★ ★

Get started here:
www.rachellechristensen.com

www.ingramcontent.com/pod-product-compliance
Lightning Source LLC
Chambersburg PA
CBHW050542190726
48284CB00003B/1182